Diana Cooper

Finn's Space Adventures

Diana Cooper

Finn's Space Adventures

Illustrated by
Kate Shannon

FINDHORN PRESS

Text © Diana Cooper 2014
Illustrations © Kate Shannon, 2014

The right of Diana Cooper and Kate Shannon to be identified as
the author and illustrator of this work has been asserted by them
in accordance with the Copyright, Designs and Patents Act 1998.

ISBN 978-1-84409-652-7

A CIP record for this title is available from the British Library.

Edited by Jacqui Lewis
Cover design and illustrations by Kate Shannon
Interior design by Damian Keenan
Printed and bound in the EU

Published by
Findhorn Press
117-121 High Street,
Forres IV36 1AB,
Scotland, UK

t +44 (0)1309 690582
f +44 (0)131 777 2711
e info@findhornpress.com
www.findhornpress.com

CONTENTS

I DEDICATE THIS BOOK
TO MY GRANDSON, FINN,
WITH LOVE.

THE KIDS MEET

Finn was bored. Another fifteen minutes to the end of class, then he could go out to play football. He yawned and brushed his blond hair away from his eyes as he gazed at the computer screen. The nine-year-old had green eyes that glowed with excitement when he was happy – so definitely not during maths. He crossed his eyes at his friend opposite him. His friend crossed his eyes back and Finn knew he was bored too. How could teachers make schoolwork so tedious? He shrugged, thinking that there could be no answer to this question, and looked out of the window.

His passion was football – well, any kind of sport. His mum would always tell him he must do well at school so he could get a good job, but he knew he was going to be a football player. 'I expect your brother will look after you in your old age,' she always added. Finn's older brother Blake was good at school, so Finn knew his mum was getting at him but he just shrugged. He was good at shrugging.

Dad would mutter, 'I wanted to be a football player at your age.' And they would give each other a sly grin of solidarity.

Dreamily he looked up at the sky and wondered what it would be like to fly – not in an aeroplane, but just fly. 'That'll never happen,' he thought. But then he did not know what the future had in store for him! He yawned and found his eyelids blinking very slowly and before he knew it his head fell forward and he was fast asleep.

In a school at the other end of the country Agapay was sitting at the back of the classroom worrying about her mum. She had a hospital appointment today and her stepdad had a day off work to take her. Agapay's mum was often ill and could not walk very well, so Agapay, who was nine, had to look after her two little brothers aged three and two when she got home from school. No one looking at

Agapay would know she had so much responsibility, though. She was always cheerful and her long fair hair was often streaked with different colours or tied back in exotic ways. She managed to flout the school uniform rules and get away with it, partly because of her huge grin and partly because they all knew her mum was ill. Today she wore one grey school sock and one green one and her teacher was pretending not to notice.

'Only half an hour till the end of the lesson. Then I can go home and see how Mum is,' the child was thinking, when suddenly her eyelids felt very heavy and she was overcome with tiredness. She put her head on the desk and fell fast asleep. Her kind-hearted teacher thought, 'Poor child. She must be tired out with all she has to do.' And yet again she pretended not to see.

Little did either of them know what was really happening.

In Bangalore, a big town in India at the other end of the world, it was late in the evening. In a very smart house in the suburbs, Vaz was industriously doing his homework. His mother went to his and his brothers' rooms frequently to check that the three boys were working properly. In the family's minds the most important thing in the world was for the boys to go to university and get good degrees. And Vaz, who was nine years old, thought this was the most important thing in the world too. He was not encouraged to dream or be adventurous, so when he too fell asleep with his head on his books, he was shocked at what happened next.

He found himself flying through the air – yes, whooshing through the sky above the land – and then he landed with a bump in what looked like a grassy meadow. Two kids about his own age landed beside him at the same time – a girl with long fair hair and odd socks and a boy with blond hair and green eyes.

'I'm Finn,' said the blond lad, looking round, 'Wherever are we?'

'No idea,' responded the girl with blue laughing eyes. 'I'm Agapay. I fell asleep and now I'm here.'

'Me too! I'm Vaz,' said the Indian boy shyly. 'What's happening?'

Before anyone could reply they heard a resounding crash and a loud scream. For an instant they stared at each other, then Agapay and Finn started to run downhill towards the sound, closely followed by Vaz. Finn arrived first. A wooden bridge over a stream had collapsed. There were planks and struts everywhere. In the middle of it all a small boy had fallen into the water and was trapped by his leg. He was struggling to get up but the water was flowing too fast and he kept going under.

Finn didn't hesitate. He jumped in, clambered over the debris and held the boy's head above the water. Agapay and Vaz leapt in too, though Vaz did pause for a second as he wondered what his mother would say when he got home wet and muddy. Then Agapay and Vaz struggled to move the plank that was trapping the boy's leg. At last they pulled it free and as it came away Agapay slipped and was dragged under the water. Finn grabbed her while Vaz held onto the little boy.

Somehow they all helped each other out of the stream and sprawled on the bank looking wet, muddy and dishevelled.

Agapay was the first to recover. 'Let me look at your leg,' she said to the child. He moved the limb towards her and she saw that his ankle was badly bruised and bleeding.

'Can you put your weight on it?' Finn asked.

The boy tried to stand but winced with pain and collapsed. 'It could be broken,' the girl said. 'I remember when my brother broke his ankle, he couldn't put weight on it. Where do you live? We need to get help.'

The little lad was bravely trying not to cry. He pointed to a little dwelling in the distance.

Vaz was looking round at the carnage of the bridge. 'Let's make a stretcher from a plank,' he suggested. 'I think that's the best way to carry him.'

Together they made a reasonable stretcher and the little boy lay on it as they carried him between them. As they approached the house a tall slim man ran down the path towards them. He seemed strangely dressed, in a sparkling blue-green shirt. Silently he lifted the boy off the plank and ran his hand over his ankle. The boy sprang to the ground with a laugh and ran inside.

The three children stared. They felt foolish. They could have sworn the boy was badly hurt.

The tall man's bright blue eyes twinkled. 'You've passed,' he called as he turned to go in. 'All the C's. Compassion, courage and cooperation. Well done.'

And the door closed.

They did not know what happened next, but suddenly Finn found himself being shaken by his teacher, who was staring at him crossly.

Agapay was running down her front path, eager to find out about her mother's hospital appointment.

While Vaz was trying to explain to his parents how he had got mud all over his trousers.

But they all knew they had passed some sort of test and something exciting was about to happen.

CHAPTER 1

THE SHAPESHIFTING MONSTERS OF URGGL

Finn was woken by a silver light, which appeared in the corner of his bedroom. It grew brighter and brighter and he didn't know whether to hide under the duvet or sit up. He decided to sit up. A figure formed inside the light. It was a tall man in a silver-blue spacesuit. He felt powerful but not threatening and he had long blond hair and piercing blue eyes. 'Hello Finn,' he said.

Finn's voice cracked with shock. 'Hello,' he managed.

'I'm Captain Ambrose of the Space Fleet.'

Finn wondered if he was dreaming. The tall man smiled. 'It's time for you to remember who you are.'

'I'm Finn White.'

'You are Finn White – and you are much more. You have special gifts and it is time to switch them on.'

Finn's mouth fell open. He could hear the TV programme that his mother was watching downstairs and he was having this conversation. It was surreal.

The captain reached out a hand and touched Finn's shoulder. He felt an electric shock running through him. 'That's done,' the man said quite casually. 'Now you can create things from thin air.'

'What?'

'You can make things or change something for the better. First you must practise. See that truly hideous china cow on that shelf.' He pointed and Finn chuckled despite himself, for the blue china cow with pink spots had been given to him by a friend of his mother's. She often slipped him some cash, so he didn't dare 'accidentally' break it. Finn's green eyes met the captain's twinkling blue ones in a glance of understanding.

'What would you really like to do with it?' the man asked.

Before the boy had time to speak the cow seemed to jump off the shelf on to the floor, where it smashed into a jigsaw of tiny pieces. Finn gasped. 'I didn't …!'

'Yes, you did. The thought flashed into your mind and you broke the cow. You'll have to be very careful what you think when you are switched on.'

Finn registered that. 'But it's not changed for the better!'

'Hey, slow down, mate. You're a beginner. Now rebuild it.'

'How?'

'Picture it how you want it to be!'

Finn closed his eyes and tried to visualize the cow again. When he opened his eyes a strange pink and blue creature stood on the shelf, not a bit like the cow it had been!

The lad stared at it aghast. He swallowed.

'Not bad for your first time. Four legs would have been nice.' Captain Ambrose grinned.

Suddenly Finn dissolved into fits of laughter.

'Come with me. We've got an emergency on our hands and I want you to meet the team.' The man disappeared.

Finn realized he was spinning very fast; then he was sucked effortlessly through the wall into the garden and into a round silver spacecraft. There were two kids about his age and a black cat sitting there. The children looked as dazed as he felt … and then Finn started to remember this strange dream he'd had during maths at school a few days ago. Or had it been a dream? Whatever it had been, these two had been there. He had met them before!

Recognition was dawning on their faces too.

'Hello again,' he said, his voice gruff with anxiety.

'Hello, Finn,' answered Agapay, who had a pink scarf tied round her neck and a matching pink streak in her blonde curls.

The boy, whose name was Vaz, Finn remembered, looked more hesitant but smiled shyly in greeting.

'Have you got gifts?' asked Finn.

'I've got the ability to talk to animals and all creatures wherever they are from,' Agapay responded.

The black cat was watching them intently. The girl looked at him and added, 'He says his name's Night and he's looking after us.' The cat nodded. The boys gulped.

'I'm told I can make people and things invisible but I haven't managed to do it yet,' Vaz admitted.

Finn felt more relaxed. 'I've got the ability to create things or rebuild something better, but all I've done so far is turned a china cow into a monster.'

They laughed.

Captain Ambrose appeared. 'All ready?' he asked seriously. 'Sorry about the lack of training but there's an emergency and we need to send you on a mission.'

They all went rather pale.

'Mission?' queried Finn.

'Yes. You're to go to another universe to an asteroid called Urrgl, where the energy is very dark. It's been invaded and the creatures who live there will be exterminated if we don't help.'

'Why us?'

'We can't slow down our frequency to their level, so we have to send you. Remember you're not to harm anything. No time to waste.' To their shock they all found themselves wearing silver spacesuits. Agapay untied her pink scarf and retied it elegantly on top of her new outfit.

Captain Ambrose continued, 'You've got all the skills you need as long as you work together. To direct your craft go into the cockpit and type your destination into the computer. Support each other – and good luck.' And he vanished.

None of them moved for a while. At last Finn said, 'Let's go.' They all rose and ran towards the cockpit where there was a huge screen and Agapay typed in URGGL. There was a whirr and seconds later a thud as they landed. Across the screen they could see the words ARRIVED AT DESTINATION URGGL.

They peered out at a grey shadowy world and were about to open the door when Agapay called out, 'Night says there's danger! He says move the craft to the other side of the hill.' Suddenly they saw a pack of huge one-eyed monsters charging towards their spaceship.

Heart thumping, Finn typed. OTHER SIDE OF THE HILL and to their relief they heard a whirr and a moment later found themselves there.

'Cool,' gasped Finn, despite the fact that he was dizzy with excitement and fear.

This time when they opened the door they saw furry creatures the size of rabbits, with huge eyes, scuttling nervously about in front of a cave mouth. About twenty metres away they could make out the outline of some shaggy-looking bushes.

'Let me try to talk to them,' offered Agapay. Nervously they descended the steps and walked towards the animals.

The girl concentrated on them for some time, then clenched her hands in frustration. She called to the cat. 'Can you help?'

Agapay listened to Night, then nodded. 'Okay you two. Focus with me and I'll try again.'

This time the boys supported her and she received information from the creatures. It was obviously not good news. She looked as grey as this strange world when she spoke again.

'Those creatures are called fizzits and they really need help. Some of those bushes over there are the shapeshifting monsters who have invaded Urggl.' To their consternation they saw that the 'bushes' had moved unnoticed towards them in the gloom.

Agapay went on, 'The fizzits eat the leaves of the genuine bushes but the monsters can change shape so realistically that it fools them and they get caught and eaten.'

Suddenly the 'bushes' transformed into huge one-eyed beasts and charged towards them. Quick as a flash the fizzits vanished into a cave. The three kids realized they were cut off from the craft, so they raced for the cave mouth and dived into the small dark entrance just in time.

'That was close,' gasped Agapay.

'If they shapeshift into snakes they can get in here,' panted Vaz.

'Sh! They're not intelligent enough to think of that but they'll pick up your thought and do it!' Finn spoke urgently. 'I've had an idea. There's no colour in this land so I'll try to turn that bush pink.' He pointed to a bush that hadn't moved.

They could hear the monsters grunting and scratching outside. Finn's hands were clammy as he hissed, 'Support me.' He pictured Agapay's bright pink scarf and focused on the tree becoming that colour. It worked! Suddenly, in the dusky gloom, the tree lit up like a pink light bulb.

The effect was extraordinary. The big black monsters backed away snarling and then fled, while the fizzits poured out of their caves and ran chattering excitedly towards the bright pink bush.

The children emerged from the smelly cave. 'The monsters are scared of light and colour,' said Agapay, 'so can you make more of it, Finn? We'll support you.' Finn thought of their Christmas tree at home and pictured the remaining bushes lighting up just like it. To his relief and astonishment, four trees suddenly started to blaze with multicoloured light. The little fizzits were ecstatic.

'You know,' commented Finn, 'Those fizzits have lived in a shadowy world for ages and now they are eating from the coloured leaves. I think the colour will help them feel happier.'

'Yes,' agreed Agapay excitedly. 'But the monsters are scared of light and colour so it will be too uncomfortable for them to be here and they'll move on.'

Vaz interrupted: 'If I can make us invisible we could get near the monsters and Agapay could try to persuade them to go.' There was a nervous silence.

'Right,' agreed Agapay rather shakily. 'I'll have a go if you really think you can make us invisible.'

Vaz explained. 'I have a special spell and the more light and colour there is the easier it is.'

'First I'll focus on creating a ball of coloured light so that we can all see,' said Finn, who was getting more confident. 'Then we'll talk to the monsters.'

It was agreed.

Finn concentrated very hard, picturing a huge multicoloured flashing ball. He was excited when red, blue and green started to shimmer and glow in front of them, then suddenly a bright light appeared. He moved it with his mind towards the howling monsters, who backed away in terror.

Next Vaz used his special spell and suddenly the three of them disappeared. It was eerie to feel Vaz's invisible hands take each of theirs. Linked together, they walked cautiously towards the pack of snarling beasts.

When they were near they stopped. Agapay tried to communicate with the creatures but they were so angry and afraid that they roared and growled. She continued to speak calmly to them, as if they were her little brothers, and at last the biggest one grunted, 'Who are you and where are you?'

'We're here to help you,' Agapay told them. 'And you would be safer and happier on your home planet.'

'Huh,' snarled the biggest one. 'No one wanted us.'

Another huffed, 'They said we were teenage thugs and were out of control.'

'They told us to find somewhere else to live.'

Agapay listened and made sympathetic sounds even though she thought they sounded horrible.

Finally they stopped ranting and she said gently, 'You sound as if you have been hurt very badly.'

'Yrrr!' they roared in agreement.

'But your families may have changed their minds by now.'

The monsters shuffled as if they would like to believe that but weren't sure.

But Agapay was very persuasive. She told them that they had changed as a result of their adventures and that their families would be delighted to see them at home again.

It was what the terrified beasts wanted to hear and before long they agreed to teleport back to the planet they belonged to. The three kids watched them rise up into the air together like a big black cloud and zoom quickly out of sight.

'Whew,' they gasped as one.

As the monster cloud disappeared the invisibility spell broke and the trio raced for the spacecraft. Once inside they waved goodbye to the furry fizzits, who completely ignored them.

'Huh! A bit of appreciation would be nice,' said Vaz in disgust.

Finn frowned. 'It sure would,' he agreed. 'We saved their lives.'

But Agapay explained that the fizzits were so stressed they couldn't think about anything apart from themselves. And the boys could understand that. They shrugged and waved again anyway.

Then they high-fived each other with sheer delight before they turned to the computer and focused on home.

CHAPTER 2

THE SUPER-VOLCANO

The familiar silver-blue light woke Finn and he sat up quickly. 'Hello Captain Ambrose,' he said, grinning, even before the spaceman had fully materialized.

The tall figure smiled a greeting. 'Hello Finn. We have another mission for you. Agapay and Vaz are waiting for you.' Finn's heart thumped with excitement and instantly he felt himself whirling through the wall of his bedroom into the spaceship.

His two new friends were sitting there in their spacesuits. To-night Agapay had a blue streak in her hair and a matching blue scarf round her neck. The children greeted each other happily.

Captain Ambrose was not smiling now. 'We have a problem,' he announced. 'And we need your assistance.'

The three nodded. They felt quite anxious as they waited to hear about their mission. The captain continued. 'A super-volcano is about to erupt on a small asteroid and the people there are in great danger. We are asking you to go there to transfer them to a place where they will be safe. We can't connect with them because their frequency is too low.'

Finn's stomach clenched. 'How long do we have before it erupts?'

'Four hours.' Captain Ambrose was crisp. 'Your craft is pro-grammed to go to Asteroid Aap as soon as I leave. You'll need to use your special gifts, so I'm switching you on now.'

He glanced at Finn, who nodded that he was ready. He and his new friends felt the current go through them as they were switched on.

'Remember to support each other,' the captain said and van-ished.

Immediately they felt the whirr of the spacecraft, and seconds later there was a slight bump and they landed on soft moss. A vast black volcano, belching thick smoke and shooting out tongues of flame, loomed in front of them.

'The volcano,' gasped Finn.

'It's huge,' squeaked Agapay. Vaz was silent with shock. It was so much bigger and fiercer than any of them had envisaged.

'Come on. Let's get out and see what we can do,' declared Finn, sounding braver than he felt.

'Just a sec.' Agapay put a hand on his arm to stop him opening the door. 'Let's ask Night for help.' The girl turned to the black cat and asked humbly, 'Have you any advice?'

She listened, then said to the boys, 'Night says to be as quick as we can. Apparently there's a twin asteroid below and very near that the people could live on but there's no food on it, so they'll have to take the moss they eat with them and grow it on the new asteroid.'

The boys digested this information, then Finn flung open the door and jumped onto the spongy green surface of the asteroid, followed by the others.

The people of the asteroid were tiny, only about fifty centimetres tall, with big heads and long arms. Hordes of them were rushing towards the spacecraft, waving, calling, crying and pointing to the volcano.

'Agapay, what are they saying?' Finn shouted urgently over the clamour. The girl tuned in to the little people. 'They want us to ferry them down to their twin asteroid.'

'We'd never do it in time,' gasped Vaz as more and more tiny figures surrounded them.

'Tell them we need to think what to do,' said Finn, but when Agapay told the people a loud groan went up, for they wanted help instantly.

'Ask who is their leader,' commanded Finn. In response to Agapay's question a much taller person, almost a metre tall, stepped forward to talk to them. Finn greeted him with a heavy heart, because he had already realized that they couldn't possibly save them all.

Just then a small child, about fifteen centimetres tall, toddled up to him. He had huge solemn black eyes and a shock of spiky red hair and he held his wee arms out to be picked up. Finn bent down and lifted up the child, who felt warm and sweet. The little boy said something that sounded like, 'Eeemoonaatee!' Agapay translated it as 'Please help!'

Finn felt terrible. He could see tears running down Agapay's cheeks and knew she felt that there was no hope. But as he looked at the blue streak in her hair like a long stream of energy with a blue slide in it, an extraordinary idea formed in his mind.

'Please ask the leader to take us to a place where we can see the twin asteroid,' he whispered to Agapay.

The tall man beckoned them to follow and the mass of people parted to let them through. He ran with the children close behind him to a long rocky ledge. From here they could see the other asteroid many miles away below them.

As they stood there they could hear loud cracks from the volcano and saw molten red rocks starting to spew out of the top. It was quite terrifying and the smell was acrid and sulphurous. The little people were in a frenzy of panic and the children didn't feel too happy either.

Finn explained his idea. 'I can build things with my thoughts, so I'm going to create a huge slide with my mind from this asteroid down to that one.'

His two friends gasped in amazement, but Vaz said at once. 'We'll support you. Do you think you can do it?'

'Can you think of anything better?' Finn asked. They shook their heads.

Agapay explained the plan to the leader, who looked shocked yet hopeful. The girl added firmly that everyone must fetch food, then form a line.

The leader explained that they ate moss stew boiled by the heat of the volcano.

'Tell them to gather moss to plant. We'll think how to stew it later,' Finn said. The leader instructed his people, while Finn used all his power to picture a slide between the two asteroids. Vaz and Agapay concentrated with him.

Nothing happened! Finn was sweating with the effort of focusing so hard. Then it appeared – the longest, widest, bluest slide in the universe.

Quickly the first of the little people, carrying armfuls of moss and babies, jumped onto it. The kids could hear their screams as they plunged very fast through space to their new home. They screamed again as they flew over a bump and Finn realized he had pictured Agapay's hair with the hairslide in it –the slide had made the bump!

Finn handed the red-haired child to his mother and felt a leap of joy as he watched them zip down the slide.

Suddenly an awful thing happened. As the child jolted over the bump he flew up into the air. His mother screamed and tried to catch him but it was too late. As the tiny red-haired boy came down he just managed to catch hold of the edge of the slide, where he hung on with his legs floating in space. He screamed too, louder than his mother.

Finn's stomach fell into his boots and he felt icy all over. Without pausing for thought he stopped any more people from getting on the slide and shouted, 'Vaz, hold my legs!' as he reached down as far as he could. It was not far enough. Vaz was heavier than Finn was, so he too lay down and inched forward holding Finn's legs. At last Finn grabbed the petrified little red-haired boy and put him back on the slide.

As Vaz pulled Finn back he could see the child reach the other asteroid, where he was hugged by his mother. Phew!

Precious time was being wasted but Finn knew he had to change the slide. Was it better to construct a fence with his mind or flatten the bump? Agapay read his mind. 'Flatten it if you can, Finn. People are frightened of what might happen to them.'

He nodded and started to focus on the slide being flat. Vaz and Agapay sat by him supporting him as he visualized it. 'You've done it, Finn!' they shouted as they saw the bump slowly smooth out. 'Well done.'

And they all jumped up to get on with the task.

The trio were feeling hotter and could see that the volcano was getting fierier by the moment. The people waiting to leave were howling and bawling in panic.

Vaz had an idea. 'I'll try to make the top of the volcano invisible,' he offered. 'If they can't see it perhaps they won't be so terrified.'

'That's a huge thing to do!' exclaimed Agapay.

'But a good idea,' added Finn.

Vaz raced towards the flaming mountain. 'Support me,' he shouted over his shoulder. He clambered part of the way up the hill. Finn and Agapay concentrated on him. Suddenly the top of the volcano vanished. The people stared, awestruck, but their fear quickly vanished and they seemed to be getting onto the slide faster and more smoothly.

Though they couldn't see the flames now that the top of the volcano had disappeared, they could still feel the fierce heat and hear the crash of rocks.

The leader insisted on being the last to leave. 'How long do we have?' asked Vaz.

'Half an hour,' Finn responded through gritted teeth. He was so hot that sweat was running down his face, leaving white streaks in the volcano dust.

'Hurry! Hurry!' he shouted, glancing over his shoulder as a boulder crashed down the mountain and landed near the spacecraft. What if it was destroyed?!

He yelled, 'It's wide enough for two at a time. Get in pairs!' Agapay quickly explained. That made the exodus faster but then the top of the volcano came into view again and everyone started screaming and pushing. The children were sweating with fear as well as heat.

At last only the leader was left. He shook each of them by the hand. 'Gowgow,' he said and they knew that meant thank you. 'Wroglip oo!' he cried and jumped onto the slide. They watched him hurtling down towards his new home.

They were all safe.

'Mission accomplished!' yelled Finn as they raced for the craft.

They threw themselves inside and instructed the computer to move the spaceship to a safe distance. Seconds later they watched as the whole volcano exploded into a great fountain of flame.

Some of the red-hot lava landed on the Aaps' new asteroid but no one was hurt.

'Great, they've got fire to cook their moss soup,' sighed Finn in relief. 'By the way, Agapay, what does "Wroglip oo" mean?'

She flushed. 'It means "You are heroes!"' she translated.

And then they were home. Finn whirred back to his bedroom and snuggled into bed. 'I really am a hero,' he thought as his eyes closed.

He was woken by his mum yanking back his duvet and crying, 'Finn, you are absolutely filthy. However did you get covered in dust? Get up and have a shower right now.'

'All right, Mum,' he murmured meekly.

CHAPTER 3

THE GIANT SPIDERS

Finn, Vaz and Agapay teleported at the same instant into the spacecraft, where Captain Ambrose was waiting. His blue eyes scanned them as he smiled. 'Ready for another adventure?' he enquired cheerfully.

'Yes, Captain Ambrose,' they replied together. Finn felt the usual twinge of fear mingled with excitement. 'Whatever could it be now?' he wondered to himself.

'It's another invasion in a different universe, I'm afraid. We need humans to help. This time giant spiders are capturing and eating the inhabitants of an island called Pddeepo and this must be stopped.'

'Giant spiders?' quavered Agapay. She did not like ordinary insects very much, let alone giant spiders.

'How big?' queried Finn. He and Vaz weren't that keen on giant spiders either.

'A couple of metres.'

'Two metres!' they all gasped.

'You must be joking!' said Finn. But Captain Ambrose wasn't joking.

Finn saw how pale Agapay was and put his hand on her arm to reassure her.

'I'll have to come with you to talk to them, I suppose?' she asked, hoping she would be let off, but the captain nodded. 'You are a team and you'll all need to use your gifts. And I'll give you something to take with you – to use only if needed.'

He handed Finn a spray can. 'This dissolves their webs,' he informed them gravely. To Agapay he gave a tube of ointment. 'For spider bites. Take care of it.'

Bites! From a two-metre-long spider! She trembled as she took the tube.

'Remember there is always a peaceful way to resolve situations without anyone getting hurt,' Captain Ambrose reminded them.

They all nodded.

There was a flash of light as the captain disappeared. The children's spacesuits materialized onto them like magic. The craft whirred. Then there was a slight bump and they saw on the computer screen ARRIVED AT DESTINATION PDDEEPO.

The three of them ran to look out of the window. Agapay let out a scream. The boys jumped back. The craft was surrounded by enormous hairy black spiders. Suddenly one of them jumped up and they could hear it scrabbling on the roof of the craft.

'What can we do?' gasped Vaz.

'Dunno but we've got to find a way,' responded Finn, though his voice shook a little. As they looked at each other in desperate silence they could hear the spiders crawling all over the spaceship.

'I'm not going out there,' Agapay announced at last, with determination in her voice.

'We'll have to be invisible,' declared Finn. 'Can you do it, Vaz?'

Vaz had been practising his gift of making things and people invisible. He felt quite confident now, and he nodded. He touched Finn and Agapay and they disappeared. Then he vanished too.

'Now to get out.' Finn opened the door a crack, then slipped out without touching any of the spiders. Vaz followed him.

They could see that the spiders were restless. They sensed something strange was happening. One jumped about ten metres and nearly landed on Finn, who dodged away just in time.

Agapay was terrified. She tried to follow the others but she stumbled as she jumped out of the spaceship and dislodged a stone. The spiders all spun round towards the sound and she leapt back into the spacecraft. Before she could shut the door a hairy leg pushed through the opening, followed by the rest of its body. It was huge with black glittering eyes and it smelled of rotten flesh. She shrank away even though she knew she was still invisible.

Because Finn and Vaz were invisible they couldn't see each other. Finn realized that they needed to be close in order to act together, so very cautiously he picked up a stone. Vaz saw it moving all by itself and realized what was happening. He crept towards his friend, who threw the stone away from the craft. It landed with a crash and the spiders raced towards it.

Vaz grabbed Finn with relief.

'Look there in the trees,' whispered Vaz. They saw rows of cocoons hanging on the branches. 'Oh my goodness,' gasped Finn. 'It's the people who have been captured by the spiders. They've spun cocoons round them.'

'What are we going to do?'

Finn thought. 'First let's throw lots of stones to lure the spiders away from the trees.'

With one accord they pelted stones as Finn directed and the spiders surged towards the commotion and milled suspiciously around.

'What now?' Vaz asked quietly.

Inside the spacecraft the spider was exploring. It moved towards the flashing light on the computer and accidentally pressed a button with one of its legs.

'No!' gasped Agapay in horror as the door closed silently. There was a familiar whirring sound and the craft streaked away.

The spider pounced towards the sound she had uttered, then, in mid-leap, it sagged and started floating around. She realized that without a spacesuit it could not cope with the change of pressure and gravity.

Finn and Vaz heard the whirr and saw the spacecraft disappear. They both went white with shock. They knew Agapay would not have left them deliberately, so what had happened? A million horrifying thoughts went through their minds, but Finn knew they must not panic. The fact was that they were here in this strange place on their own – but he had to believe that Agapay would return with the spacecraft.

'I've got an idea,' he said at last. 'I'll build a huge mirror facing the spiders and perhaps that will confuse them while we free the people from the cocoons.'

'Will you be able to materialize something as big as that without Agapay's energy?' Vaz asked doubtfully. Finn just said simply, 'We'll have to do our best.' They concentrated as hard as they could and soon a mirror appeared, ten metres high and twenty metres long, facing towards the spiders.

The boys crept towards the trees.

'I've got the dissolving spray,' whispered Finn. He aimed at the bottom of a cocoon and rather to their surprise, the end just melted away and a little man tumbled out, looking rather dazed. Finn ran down the row spraying the cocoons and more and more people slipped out of them. He realized that there were hundreds of them.

Now they could hear a terrible commotion from the other side of the mirror, which was shaking and crashing. Finn realized that the spiders thought their reflections were enemy spiders and were throwing themselves at the glass!

At home on Planet Earth several things happened at once. There was a bump as the craft with Agapay and the spider inside it landed. The word HOME flashed onto the screen. The girl became visible again – she was out of range of Vaz's spell. The spider collapsed into a corner.

Immediately Agapay felt huge compassion. Forgetting it might bite, she ran over to the insect and tried to communicate. Spider language was difficult and this creature was very groggy and terrified.

Nevertheless, a few moments later when Captain Ambrose entered the craft, he found Agapay kneeling by the giant female spider, gently offering it sips of water. She explained to the captain that the spider was telling her they were all afraid there would not be enough food, so they captured everything they could, even each other. This meant that none of them felt safe any more. Agapay told it she understood and if it came back with her they would find a way of helping them all to feel safe. She hoped that they would be able to, but she knew she must go back for Finn and Vaz anyway.

Captain Ambrose nodded to her and vanished as Agapay typed DESTINATION PDDEEPO into the computer.

The boys heard a whirr and to their huge relief the craft landed beside them. They rushed forward to find out what had happened and to see if Agapay was all right. The door opened and they fell back in horror and shock, staring open-mouthed as a giant spider emerged with Agapay riding on his back.

The spider was distraught that all their prey had escaped, but Agapay reminded her gently that they were not supposed to eat people and that there was plenty of different food to be had.

They could hear the enraged spiders climbing up the other side of the mirror. They would soon be over it.

Agapay called, 'Finn and Vaz! I can't see you. Where are you? I need to talk to you.'

The boys made themselves visible again.

'What is it? Where have you been?' asked Finn, warily eyeing the spider on which his friend was riding.

Agapay replied, 'She won't hurt you, will you, Spiderdoodle?'

'Is that her name?' scoffed Vaz, crossing his eyes to indicate he thought it stupid, but Agapay said quickly. 'The other spiders will hurt you if they get you but I've discovered they are afraid of fire and water.'

'Thanks, that's great,' said Finn. 'We'll have to protect the people from the spiders until they are ready to live in harmony. Come on. Let's all get to work before the spiders realize what is happening.'

Agapay communicated with the people that they were to build a fire. While some were digging a trench others would carry flaming branches and form a moving line of fire to protect them from the spiders. They set to work.

Spiderdoodle rolled her eyes and reared up at the sight of the flames, so Agapay slid off her back and she bounded away.

The people told Agapay that there used to be a big river running across the middle of the island but the spiders had blocked the source, in the mountains. That was when their troubles started. So a group set off, protected by fire-bearers, to unblock the source of the river.

Meanwhile Agapay, Finn and Vaz treated everyone's spider bites with the ointment Captain Ambrose had given them. People who had been sick and listless were soon running about and able to help.

Before long everyone cheered – a trickle of water was running along the dry river bed. It became a stream, then a river and finally a torrent. The spiders had discovered the mirror was a trick and they streamed over it towards the river. There they stopped. Rows of them stood staring at the water.

Then Spiderdoodle stood on a fallen log and addressed them all. Agapay couldn't hear what she said but she had a feeling that the giant spider was asking them all to act differently in future, and that they were willing to.

As for the people, they were very grateful. They wanted to hold a feast in honour of their saviours but the three children said that they had to go home or else they would be late for their supper and their mums would be cross.

CHAPTER 4

The Baby Spiders Cause Havoc

It was the last week of the summer holidays. Finn knew that Agapay and her family were due home from their trip to France today. He hoped she'd had a good time and smiled as he thought of her colourful hair and cheeky smile. He could see a clear picture of her in his mind – and suddenly he found himself whirling through the air. Next thing he was standing on the drive of a small house and there on a low wall sat Vaz.

'Hi Vaz!' said Finn. 'What are you doing here? Where are we?'

'I guess this is Agapay's house. I was thinking about her and suddenly found myself here,' replied Vaz.

'Me too,' agreed Finn. They were used to strange happenings by now, but this was bizarre. 'We must have apported.' Captain Ambrose had explained to them that this was when someone made themselves turn up somewhere just by visualizing and willing themselves there.

Vaz shrugged. 'What shall we do now? It doesn't look as if she's here.' At that moment, though, a blue hatchback turned in to the drive, its wheels crunching on the gravel. Agapay, in the back seat, saw them at once and jumped out of the car as soon as it stopped with a look of surprise and delight on her face. 'What are you two doing here?' she called, tossing back her orange and yellow hair.

They did not have time to reply, because a man – Agapay's stepdad – opened the front door – and screeched as two giant spiders squeezed past him, almost knocking him down. They were not as huge as Spiderdoodle but must have been two metres wide. The hungry predators loped off in the direction of the village, leaving Agapay's stepdad looking shocked. Her mum, who was still in the car, screamed and her little brothers howled.

'Spiderdoodle must have laid eggs,' gasped Agapay.

'And they've hatched,' finished Finn grimly.

'Have you still got the web-dissolving spray and bite ointment?' asked Vaz. The girl nodded and ran into the house, calling, 'Wait there for me.'

She was out again in seconds and, ignoring the shouts of Agapay's parents, the three children hared after the giant spiders.

The village main street was a scene of chaos. Two cars had collided in the middle of the road and their terrified occupants were trapped inside, not daring to move. Other cars were slewed across the street, their doors wide open – their drivers and passengers had run to the shops for refuge. The shopping centre was deserted except for the two giant spiders. Frightened faces peeped out of shop doors or stared out of windows.

One of the spiders had a red spot on its back. It sidled over to a lamp post and started to spin a web, each thread thick as rope, right across the road. As the children watched from behind a tree, the web grew so quickly that it soon blocked the street completely.

In the meantime the second spider, which had blue-spotted legs, ran to the two cars that had crashed and leapt onto them. It danced what looked like a war dance on the cars' roofs.

Agapay gasped. 'That's Miss Sharp in there. She's the meanest teacher in the school. She bullies the little ones. Nasty old bat.'

When the spider jumped off the car in search of something more interesting, Agapay ran over to the car. There was a gasp of horror from the onlookers when they saw her. She whipped out her phone and took pictures of the woman behind the wheel, whose mouth was wide open as she screamed in terror. That done, Agapay pocketed her phone with a smile of satisfaction and scuttled back to rejoin the boys.

Just then Agapay's stepdad raced from his hiding place behind a wall and grabbed her arm. 'Come home, Agapay, you silly child,' he yelled and started to pull her away. Finn and Vaz's eyes met and Vaz instantly made all three of them invisible. Agapay's stepdad looked shocked and bewildered as she vanished. Automatically he loosened his grip on her invisible arm and she squirmed away.

Finn and Vaz grabbed her hands, or where they guessed her hands would be, and together they crept towards the spiders.

'I've got to talk to them,' whispered Agapay. 'They'll listen to me.'

But at that moment the starving spiders spotted a foolish ginger and white cat, who had let curiosity overcome common sense and was sitting in the road nearby, watching. As one they charged after the animal, who took off at a run. A scream from a dress shop pierced the air and a plump lady in a red blouse hammered on the window. 'Ginger, my Ginger!' she screeched. Even though the cry came from indoors, everyone could hear her and it made the villagers' blood run cold.

The cat veered in desperation towards the sound of her mistress's voice but the blue-spotted spider pounced and bit the unfortunate creature, who howled, then lay on the ground twitching.

Agapay put her hand to her mouth in distress. 'I've got the bite cream,' she murmured. 'I've got to help.' Letting go of the boys' hands, she crept towards where Ginger the cat lay, but just then the two spiders decided to fight over their meal and she could not get near the animal for rolling bodies and flailing legs.

'Divert them,' she pleaded to the invisible boys and they picked up gravel and some litter. They pelted the two spiders, who paused in their fight for a moment to see who their common enemy was. The courageous Agapay saw them pause, hurried through their legs to the injured cat and spread the ointment onto the animal's wound. Ginger stirred, then suddenly leapt up and raced for her cat flap, so quickly that it caught the spiders off guard. The moment they realized they pounced together, just missing Agapay, and crashed in mid-air just as the cat reached safety. The hungry insects stared at each other crossly.

Now everyone could hear Ginger's owner squealing with delight as she hugged her pet nearly to death. Then everyone in the shop examined in wonder the red bite on the cat's neck, covered in strange sticky cream. But Ginger seemed fine and even purred, so they turned their attention back to the spiders.

The one with the red spot hurried to the centre of its web, from where it glowered menacingly at the occupants of the two cars that had collided. They shrank away from it. Agapay would have liked another photo.

The blue-spotted spider had caught a whiff of meat from the

butcher's shop. It ran towards the smell and started to batter the glass shop door with its long legs. Eventually it broke a small window at the top, thrust a two-metre hairy leg through and grabbed a pork chop. It pulled it back through the broken window and devoured it. When it put its tentacle-like leg through the window once more to steal another morsel the burly butcher, who had been cowering at the back of his shop, became enraged as he watched his profits disappear. He ran forward and grabbed the spider's tentacle as it fastened it on to another chop. The butcher tugged and the spider pulled. Everyone was screaming.

The children knew they must get help. Simultaneously they all sent a telepathic SOS to Captain Ambrose, as he had taught them.

Finn had been thinking hard. 'I'm going to create a giant metal crate to lure them into. Help me,' he said to the others. They all focused.

The hiding onlookers gasped as a vast orange and yellow metal container appeared in the middle of the road. Agapay smiled to herself, for she knew Finn had imagined the colour of the spray in her hair.

'Now it's my turn,' she declared. 'I'll talk to them.'

'They won't listen until they've both eaten,' cautioned Finn and she had to concede that he was right.

Just then they heard the wail of sirens and four police cars burst into the village street. A dozen officers jumped out. One spider relinquished its tug of war with the butcher over the pork chop and ran towards them. The other jumped down from its web and darted in their direction. Twelve police officers leapt back into their cars even more quickly than they had got out!

Vaz and Agapay started to push the crate towards the spiders while Finn dashed to the butcher's shop and demanded steaks for the insects. His disembodied voice so spooked the butcher that he threw two steaks through the broken window without argument. Finn caught them and was throwing them into the crate as a lure when, abruptly, the invisibility spell wore off. All three children became visible – and they were within metres of the spiders. The watchers screamed. Loudest of all was Agapay's mother, who struggled up from her wheelchair and tried to hobble towards her daughter. The spiders swivelled towards the children.

Immediately Agapay called out something in the strange, slithery, crawly-sounding spider language and the giant insects, which had been poised to leap on them, stood still. Unexpectedly, they both visibly relaxed. They almost seemed to shrink.

'We've come to help you and take you back to where you belong. There's food in the crate. We'll make sure you are safe,' promised the girl, in the spiders' language first and then in translation for everyone watching. If spiders could smile those two would have done so. They crawled meekly into the box and everyone could hear appreciative sucking and munching sounds as they tucked in to the steaks.

Vaz grabbed the web-dissolving spray and set to work to clear the great web, and within moments it had disappeared.

And then an extraordinary thing happened. A small spacecraft glided silently in between the rows of shops and landed neatly in front of the police cars where the web had been moments before. Out of it stepped the tall silver-clad figure of Captain Ambrose. The relieved children rushed up to him to explain.

The police officers, the people in the cars, Agapay's family and all the watching villagers gaped in disbelief.

No one moved as the space captain clicked his fingers and the orange box containing the spiders rose and glided smoothly into the craft. Captain Ambrose levitated in behind it and the two boys followed, waving goodbye to their friend Agapay.

The usually nice Agapay now did something unexpected. While everyone was still gaping in stunned silence, she ran across to the car where the nasty teacher was now glaring spitefully at her. The woman wound down the car window and was opening her mouth to reprimand her when Agapay thrust her phone at her. 'I have these pictures of you, Miss Sharp, and if you bully the little ones again I'll show them to everyone.' Miss Sharp shut her mouth abruptly and nodded. Agapay knew that the teacher's behaviour at school was about to change quite dramatically.

Just then she shivered as the spacecraft whirred past and a

strange green mist started to rise from the ground. She joined her parents and brother, who looked vague and puzzled as they made their way home in silence.

Nothing changed much after the strange day with the spiders. Only the butcher complained darkly to his customers that someone had stolen a pork chop and two steaks and Miss Sharp suddenly became very pleasant and helpful to the little ones. She seemed to be in awe of Agapay too, but no one could think why.

The headline in the local paper was about a sudden strange mist that had engulfed the village. No one knew it was a Fog of Forgetting, sent so that none of them would remember a thing.

CHAPTER 5

THE GOLDEN TRUMPET

Captain Ambrose was looking thoughtfully at the computer of the spaceship as the three kids arrived. He turned to them with a broad smile. 'Are you ready for a special quest?' he asked.

Finn's green eyes glinted with anticipation. A quest! Whatever could it be this time? He grinned at Agapay and Vaz and they all said 'Yes!' in unison.

Agapay had her ankle bandaged. She'd sprained it in a fall but she was not going to let that stop her. 'What is it?' she asked.

'We want you to go to a golden planet and bring back the Golden Trumpet.'

Questions flew round Finn's brain like a flock of birds. 'What's the Golden Trumpet?' he asked.

Captain Ambrose became serious. 'Okay, Kids. It will be a challenge. The Golden Trumpet has a specific note. It is sounded every 260,000 years throughout the universes to call volunteers to bring peace to Earth.

'But why can't you get it?' queried Vaz.

'Ah,' replied Captain Ambrose. 'It's guarded by fire dragons and only humans can face them. That's why it's a special quest.'

'Fire dragons!' exclaimed Agapay in horror.

'We'll look after you,' Finn promised her protectively. Then he gulped, 'Fire dragons!'

'It is vitally important and if you bring the Golden Trumpet home you will receive a special gift,' Captain Ambrose told them.

That sounded good but whatever could it be? They already had their individual gifts, of course: Finn could make things materialize with his thoughts, Agapay could communicate with all species and Vaz could make people invisible.

Still wondering to themselves what this new gift could be, the children nodded to show that they would accept the challenge.

With that, they instantly found themselves in their spacesuits.

The captain smiled, tapped something on the computer, then vanished. The craft whirred. The children felt a slight movement and then a bump. As they landed the screen said ARRIVED DESTI-NATION GOLDEN EARTH.

Through the window of the craft they could see a beautiful, bright world. Trees shimmered emerald. Fountains sparkled like diamonds. Flowers radiated a million colours.

Tall people appeared outside the craft like magic. Golden light glowed round them and all were smiling a welcome.

Finn pressed the button to open the door of the spacecraft. As they stepped into the new world they immediately felt happy and optimistic. 'Wow!' exclaimed Agapay as light from the welcome party reached out and surrounded her. It made her feel so good.

A boy stepped forward and showed Finn what looked like a small watch on his arm. It turned out to be a tiny computer, infinitely more powerful than anything he had ever seen. Agapay translated for the kid. 'It responds to thoughts. If you want some information, you think about it and the answer appears in a bubble above the computer.'

'Wow!' exclaimed Finn and Vaz. This was a computer infinitely more powerful than the ones they knew.

The boy laughed at their incredulity. Then he paused and listened. 'My mum's calling me for lunch. Got to go. Bye.' He vanished.

A lady with long fair hair explained, 'We're all telepathic. His mother called him and he has teleported home.'

'Teleported?' asked Finn.'

'Yes. You think yourself somewhere and go there instantly.'

'Wow,' they exclaimed again.

'You have moved into your future. This is Earth in 2050. Everything is high-frequency with a golden aura.'

They looked at her open-mouthed as it registered properly with them that they had moved through time.

The lady then turned to Agapay. 'Is your ankle painful?'

The girl nodded with a grimace. The golden light expanded

round the woman as she pointed a crystal at Agapay's leg. Then she uttered a harmonious low note. Agapay let out a gasp. 'The pain's gone! My ankle's better. How did you do that?'

'We can heal anything with crystals and the right notes.'

'Thank you, thank you,' laughed Agapay in delight. Then she looked sad for a moment as she thought of her mum. 2050 was too long to wait.

'We came here for the Golden Trumpet,' said Finn. The lady smiled and pulled a sheet of paper out of thin air. 'I was expecting you. Here is a map for your quest.'

Finn took it and the children looked at it eagerly. There was a mountain with a dot on it, a river, a forest and a star.

The lady said, 'A word of advice: listen to your intuition. It's not going to be easy but it is full moon tonight.' And she disappeared.

The children looked at each other. 'What does that mean?' whispered Agapay. The boys shrugged. They did not know either.

Finn studied the map again. 'Let's go to the mountain,' he announced. 'Look, it's over there.' They couldn't understand why they hadn't seen it before because it was looming over them. They set off eagerly towards it.

'We'll have to cross this river first,' pointed out Vaz as they reached a wide, deep, slow-moving river.

'I've never seen such clear water,' murmured Agapay. 'You can see everything at the bottom.'

'Look at those fish!' Finn indicated the brightly coloured fish that were swimming towards them. 'Talk to them, Agapay. Find out where we can cross the river. Is there a bridge?'

Agapay sent a telepathic question to the fish and listened. Then she looked puzzled. 'They said, "Call a boat,"' she reported.

'Of course, I'll manifest one.' Finn concentrated hard and a big old rowing boat appeared right in front of them. Vaz and Agapay roared with laughter. 'Not on the grass, Finn. We need it on the river. It's too heavy to move.'

Finn blushed. He didn't think it was the least bit funny. It took a lot of effort to build things from thin air.

'She said to call a boat, not make one,' said Agapay. 'It would be great if we called and a boat just came along.' And as she uttered the words a magnificent, streamlined cream and blue boat floated down the river towards them. It stopped nearby and gently bumped the bank as if inviting them to get in.

They scrambled in, almost tipping it over, and it floated silently towards the opposite bank. The three children were so intent on getting there that they scarcely noticed anything in their surroundings and didn't speak to one another. They had almost reached the other side when three large pink fish leapt out of the water in front of them. The boat stopped.

The fish were opening and closing their mouths. Agapay translated: 'They say we are too serious. We must lighten up.'

One of the fish squirted water at Finn and drenched him. He felt irritated and frowned. Immediately the fish tipped the boat over and the three children fell into the water! They spluttered as they surfaced. Agapay had a long piece of weed hanging from her hair. To their surprise the fish stood on their tails and their mouths opened wide. Agapay didn't need to translate that they were roaring with laughter.

Suddenly the children saw how funny it was and they all started laughing too.

One fish said something to Agapay, who told the others, 'It says "A quest starts with purification".'

She thought for a moment and then said, 'Of course. Laughter purifies and so does water. We were too serious so we got the water treatment.' The fish nodded happily.

Vaz brightened up. 'So we really are going in the right direction?'

'Looks like it.' Finn scrambled out of the water and peered up the mountain. 'I can see a cave up there past that wood. I bet that's the dot on the map. Let's go.'

As they climbed up the slope in their dripping clothes they waved to people who were watching them, including the lady they had spoken to earlier. Although it was steep it didn't take as long as they had expected to reach the wood. But it was more like a forest, gloomy and dark.

Agapay took a step back. 'It doesn't feel good,' she whispered. 'It's scary.'

'It's not very big,' murmured Vaz doubtfully.

But Finn said, 'Come on. Let's go for it.' And he stepped onto a path and promptly tripped over a bramble. 'I swear it jumped up to get me,' he muttered angrily as he got up.

Agapay couldn't help it. She giggled and the boys found themselves laughing too. As soon as they laughed the path seemed lighter and they heard a bird singing.

'I'll go first this time,' announced Vaz and strode off. They told each other silly jokes so that they laughed all the way, and soon the path opened out into the most beautiful magical glade. There was a little twinkling stream with stepping-stones across it, brightly coloured flowers tumbled everywhere and the trees were light-filled and pale green. The sun poured into the clearing, not too hot but a perfect warmth. Bizarrely, a little train, big enough to sit in, was puffing its way through the trees. There were children sitting in it and they beckoned to the three to join them.

'Come on,' shouted Finn. 'Let's have a ride.'

But Agapay held back. She frowned doubtfully. 'Wait. We're on a quest. There's always temptation to get us off track. I think this is it.'

Finn and Vaz were both irritated. 'Don't be silly. It's fine.'

But Agapay was adamant. 'You ride on it if you want to but I'm not going to.'

Reluctantly the boys agreed that they must all stay together, but they were both very miffed and Vaz kicked at a tree stump.

And then a strange thing happened. As they walked out of the glade the train and the children simply vanished. No one said anything but the boys realized that Agapay had been right! This was no ordinary quest.

Ten minutes later they were out of the deep dark forest and halfway up the mountain. Up there ahead of them lay the cave.

They approached it very cautiously but this time it was Finn who suddenly felt very nervous. His stomach clenched and his hands felt clammy. As they peered in, they heard a terrible roar from somewhere inside the mountain. They turned and ran. When they looked back they could see flames spewing from the cave.

It was the fire dragon.

They sat disconsolately on a rock. What on earth were they to do?

'I know. I'll use my spell to make us invisible,' suggested Vaz and they agreed that was the only way. Vaz did his magic and they held hands so that they would stay together as they crept up to the cave. This time they saw the trumpet glinting on a high ledge at the back of the cave – but they also saw the shape of a huge dragon in front of it.

Even though they were invisible they paused, hearts thumping. Then they stepped cautiously inside. Immediately they heard the roar again and a lick of fire burst towards them. Letting go of each other's hands, they turned and pelted as fast as they could back down the mountain.

Sitting on the rock again and once more visible they assessed the situation. 'The dragon can see through the dimensions, so even if we are invisible in ours he can still see us,' muttered Finn gloomily.

Agapay held the map. 'Why is there a star? And why did the lady mention the full moon?' she wondered aloud. But they had no answer.

Vaz said, 'Mum always says, if you want to know something just ask.'

They looked around and saw the lady who had given them the map. She was standing some distance away, quietly watching.

'Let's ask her,' suggested Finn.

So they marched towards her and she smiled as they approached.

'Please could you tell us how to get past the dragon to get the Golden Trumpet?' asked Finn.

She shook her head. 'I can't tell you anything like that, but I can give you a hint. Quests involve purification, resisting temptation, an open heart and courage. Now just sit down and look over there.' As they sat in silence on the ground they saw that the sun was setting. The sky got darker and at last a beautiful full moon hung like a pearl in the sky.

One star shone more brightly than the others. Suddenly Agapay burst out. 'I think that's Venus.' She glanced at the lady, who said encouragingly. 'It's the star on the map. And what does Venus stand for?'

'Love!' they exclaimed together.

The lady nodded. 'Dragons respond to love. I suggest you breathe in the love from Venus into your hearts and then send it to the fire dragon.'

They felt a bit weird doing this but they looked at the star and breathed the light into their hearts, then imagined it going to the dragon. They started to feel very peaceful and their hearts felt warm.

At last Finn announced, 'My heart feels warm and open. What about you two?'

'Me too. I'm ready to try again,' agreed Agapay. She was scared but determined.

Vaz added. 'So is my heart. I'm ready. Let's go.'

Courage is about doing something even though you are terrified. They walked bravely along the path, which was lit by the moonlight. All the way they breathed in love from Venus and sent it to the dragon. At the mouth of the cave they glanced at one another, then called out together to the dragon, 'Hello.'

At this the enormous dragon emerged from the cave. This time he was not breathing fire. He just looked at them.

It was Agapay who asked. She sent a last breath of pure love to the dragon and stepped forward. 'Please may we have the Golden Trumpet?'

The huge dragon eyed her in silence. She felt as if he was looking through her and right into her heart. Then he disappeared into the cave. The three children eyed each other but no one spoke. They thought he might be able to hear their hearts hammering, though.

Seconds later the fire dragon returned. He held the Golden Trumpet in his mouth. It was magnificent and much bigger than they had imagined. 'Thank you, thank you, thank you,' said the three children as they took it gratefully from him. 'Take care of it,' the dragon said to Agapay, who translated for the others and then said, 'We will.'

They all thanked him again and said goodbye, then set off down the path carrying their precious burden. Halfway down the mountain they heard a muted roar like distant thunder and the world lit up with a great flame. It was the dragon's goodbye.

The lady met them at the bottom of the mountain. 'Well done,' she said as she greeted them. When she saw the Golden Trumpet she was awed. 'It's magnificent.' They looked at it in admiration for some time before she said that she would take them back to their craft. She touched them and they found themselves flying over the river and back to the spaceship.

When they reached home Captain Ambrose was waiting for them in the mothercraft. He was very pleased with the children and they all secretly wondered what their gift would be. With a wide smile he told them they were each going to be given their own personal fire dragon.

'A fire dragon!' they exclaimed as one. Their huge grins told him how delighted they were.

At that moment, with a roar like thunder, three bouncy young dragons burst into the craft and flew over to them. They were livelier than puppies, with wonderful shimmering wings.

One flew directly to Finn and puffed out a little smoke towards him.

'Hello Flame,' Finn welcomed him, feeling he'd known him for ever.

'Hello Finn, old friend,' replied the dragon and they grinned joyfully at each other.

'But now we must go to the highest mountain and blow the trumpet,' announced Captain Ambrose. 'Do you want to come?'

'Yes please!' they all cried and he set the computer.

A second later the captain laughed. He said, 'Look out of the window!'

They saw a thousand spacecraft following them as they streaked to the top of Mount Everest. Luckily there was no one else there as they landed on the pinnacle. A tall man in a silver and blue spacesuit stepped forward and took the Golden Trumpet. Captain Ambrose whispered to them that he was Commander Ashtar, the commander of the entire space fleet.

He placed the trumpet to his lips and sent out a clarion call that was heard throughout the universes.

The dragons flew round and round in exuberant fiery circles.

'Thank you Finn, Agapay and Vaz,' Commander Ashtar said to them. 'You have helped the world today and I'm glad you like your dragons.'

CHAPTER 6

THE FIRE DRAGONS

Finn was lying in bed when he heard a roar like thunder. He sat up quickly as a streak of orange light landed on his bed. 'Shh!' he murmured. 'You'll wake everyone up.'

Flame, his dragon, opened his mouth and said 'Sorry,' in a smoky whisper. Finn could have sworn he was grinning.

'What are you doing here? It's the middle of the night!' Finn asked him.

'Commander Ashtar sent me himself. We're needed.'

Finn felt a prickly sensation in his scalp. 'We?' he queried.

'Captain Ambrose and your spacecraft have been captured and I'm to take you to rescue them.' Flame puffed out his chest with pride and it glowed orange.

But Finn went white and his hair stood on end.

'Captured! How . . .? What happened?' he demanded. 'And what about Vaz and Agapay? Are they all right?'

In response the dragon flicked his tail and opened the curtains with one paw. Floating outside the window astride their dragons were Vaz and Agapay, waiting for him.

'Hurry up,' called Vaz when he saw them.

Finn did not quite know how it happened but in an instant he found himself wearing his spacesuit, seated on Flame and bursting through the wall to join them. Immediately the other two dragons, Pitta and Bizz, raced off with their children aboard. Finn crouched low, holding on grimly as Flame torpedoed after them.

'Where are we going?' he yelled.

'To rescue Captain Ambrose and the craft from the Martians!'

For a second Finn thought he was going to fall off in shock. He felt his stomach clench and his knees wobble.

'The Martians!' He must be dreaming. Grimly he urged Flame to go faster. If Agapay and Vaz could do this, so could he.

Lots of people looking up into the sky that night thought they saw shooting stars; they couldn't have guessed that in fact the 'stars' were three dragons carrying three brave children on a mission.

As they neared Mars, Finn called, 'Stop, you two! What's our plan?'

Vaz and Agapay drew in their dragons and they all floated in the blackness of space, staring at the red planet in front of them. All they could see was craggy, inhospitable terrain with fire and steam pouring from caves dotted here and there. It was grim.

Several spacecraft whizzed past them without noticing them. They could feel the rush of air and knew they were much too close for comfort.

Finn shivered and Flame muttered, 'Looks like hell over there,' which did nothing to help him feel better.

'Shall we go down to look for the captain?' Agapay asked in a rather wobbly voice. The boys did not reply.

'You need a plan,' said the dragons, all together.

'All right, all right. Give us a moment to think,' muttered Finn.

The three children stared at Mars, trying to make out what was going on. In the gloom they could see creatures rushing about and a big dark object.

Vaz spoke first. 'Finn can you materialize binoculars so we can see what's happening?'

'Sure,' Finn sounded more confident than he felt. He hoped Captain Ambrose had switched his gift on. He focused on creating a pair of giant binoculars with powerful lenses and was very relieved when they appeared in his hands. He put them to his eyes at once. 'That dark blob is our captured spacecraft. It's tethered with wire ropes. And it's guarded by little red creatures.'

He handed the binoculars to Agapay and she peered through them. 'I can see the same,' she agreed crisply and passed them to Vaz.

A group of spacecraft shot silently past them, clearly on a mission, and they felt a sense of foreboding.

'Vaz can you make us invisible and we'll go down,' Finn pronounced decisively. 'We have to find the captain.'

Vaz nodded. He called up his gift of making things disappear and the children vanished – but he couldn't make the dragons invisible. He was disappointed but Pitta, his dragon, put in quickly, 'Never mind Vaz. We can move very fast.' The other two nodded in agreement.

Carrying their charges, all three dived like flashes of lightning towards the surface of Mars.

Finn, Vaz and Agapay held their breaths. Then they felt a bump and quickly jumped off their dragons. Holding hands to ensure they stayed together while they couldn't see each other, they ran past the guards towards the craft. As they did so they dislodged some stones and there was a fizz as one of the guards let off a heat machine. Even though they were invisible this could still harm them, so they ran faster.

They crouched beside the spacecraft and Agapay peeped in. 'He's not there!' she gasped in dismay. 'But there are Martians examining it.'

'What are they saying?' asked Finn and Vaz with one voice, for Agapay had the gift of being able to understand all creatures.

She frowned as she concentrated. 'Tell us,' said Vaz impatiently after a few moments but she shushed him as she tried to hear what was being said.

'Okay,' she whispered at last. 'The captain is in the big dome on the other side of the craft. They are using special crystals on him to get him to reveal how the craft works. Then they will have a frying ceremony.'

'What!' exclaimed the boys in horror. The Martians were going to fry Captain Ambrose? Surely they would do the same to them if they caught them!

The guards discharged more steam towards the sound of their voices and the children ducked and ran towards the dome.

They crept past the outer row of guards, careful not to brush against one or to dislodge any more stones. But to their horror a large crowd of Martian soldiers had gathered in front of the main door. There was no way they could slip through, even though they were invisible.

Suddenly Agapay squeezed Finn's and Vaz's hands and nudged them to look up. The dragons had seen their dilemma and were creating a diversion. They were picking up boulders, making them red hot in their mouths and dropping them as close as they could to the soldiers.

Screaming and howling, the little creatures were running in all directions. The Martians who were inside the dome rushed to the entrance to see what the commotion was about and the dragons

swooped down on them as they stepped outside. They had never seen such creatures and ran away in terror.

'Let's go,' whispered Finn and the trio dropped hands and raced inside. Captain Ambrose was tied to a great stone chair in the middle of the room. He looked pale but dignified.

'It's us,' whispered Agapay. The captain acknowledged them with a slight nod of the head and the children remembered he could see through the dimensions, so he could see them even though they were invisible to each other and the Martians.

'You can't cut these cords,' the tall man murmured quietly. 'Leave me now and get to safety.'

'No sir,' responded Finn, surprising himself. He had never called anyone sir in his life.

'Absolutely not!' agreed Vaz.

Suddenly Finn was icy with determination. 'I'm going to manifest cutters that can shear through any material, known or unknown,' he announced. 'Support me, guys.'

Vaz, Agapay and the captain added their energy to Finn's as he concentrated on creating the most powerful tool he could conjure up. After a long moment a huge pair of shimmering cutters started to become visible and in that same moment guards started pouring into the room.

Finn ignored them as he set about severing the chains that bound the captain to the stone seat. As he did so the screaming guards launched themselves towards the man and in a flash Vaz rendered the captain invisible. Before he disappeared Agapay grabbed his hand. Finn and Vaz linked quickly too. The shocked guards were scrambling all over the place looking for him and Vaz hoped against hope that his invisibility spell would last. He focused hard on maintaining it.

But now the children realized just how weakened the captain was. He could hardly move. All at once Finn knew what he must do. He uttered a low whistle and pandemonium ensued as the three dragons catapulted through the doors, their wings held back like diving birds.

The Martians fell to the ground in terror, allowing the children time to help the captain onto Flame's back. Finn leapt up behind him, while Vaz jumped onto Pitta and Agapay scrambled onto Bizz. They ducked as the dragons soared through the doors and spread their wings. That was when the invisibility spell dissolved and everyone could see them.

Finn wondered what to do about the spacecraft but the captain roared. 'Leave the craft! It can be rescued later. Get us out of here.' So they rose up high and streaked through the universe back to Earth like orange rockets.

When they landed a reception committee awaited them. Captain Ambrose was taken to a healing place to rebalance and energize his systems.

To their joy and amazement Commander Ashtar, the head of the Space Fleet, appeared in a silver-blue light to shake their hands and to thank them personally.

Dawn was breaking and the first birds had started to sing as the dragons delivered three very tired but proud children back to their beds. As he fell asleep Finn felt very pleased with himself.

But his mum was not happy the next morning when she found scorch marks on his pyjamas.

'How did you get these?' she demanded crossly.

'Dunno,' the boy muttered sheepishly.

CHAPTER 7

The Flying Discs

It was a dull, drizzly December day and Finn felt bored as he stretched out on his bed playing yet another computer game.

As he yawned for the second time there was a sudden flash and Captain Ambrose flickered into the room.

'Hi!' exclaimed Finn, sitting up, his green eyes suddenly shining. 'What are you doing here?'

The captain laughed. 'Waking you up!'

Finn looked at him expectantly. When the captain appeared it usually heralded adventure, challenges and excitement. His stomach flipped and Captain Ambrose read his thoughts, responding with a smile. 'No danger today, Finn, but a challenge I think you'll enjoy!'

Finn ran his hand through his short blond hair so that it stood on end. He was bursting with curiosity, but the spaceman shook his head. 'Wait. I'll tell all three of you together.' The boy knew he meant his friends Agapay and Vaz, who went on space trips with him. The captain vanished before Finn could say another word and he felt the familiar sensation of being pulled through the wall. He found himself sitting in the spacecraft in his spacesuit.

Seconds later Agapay, who had red rose petals clipped all over her long fair hair, and Vaz, in a blue sweater, arrived in the same flash. They scarcely had time to grin a welcome to each other before their captain materialized, smiling broadly.

'You're going to school!' he announced.

'No!' the three children exploded simultaneously in disgust.

'Patience,' laughed the man, holding up a hand. 'I'm taking you to a space school – on Sirius.'

'Sirius?' exclaimed Finn, while Agapay said with a frown of surprise, 'That's a star system in this universe, isn't it?'

'Yes, it's the bright star we can often see.' Captain Ambrose said, nodding. 'You are right.' He told them there were a number of training schools on Sirius but, of course, they were in a different dimension from our physical ones. 'They are working on the technology to be brought to Earth in the future. When the Sirians have perfected it and people are ready for it here it will be passed to your scientists, who will "invent" it.'

The children glanced at each other excitedly and the captain added, 'You'll be starting with the Transport Department to learn about the vehicles of the future.'

'What do you want us to do?' asked Agapay.

'We want you to go there to observe and offer your human perspective. Okay?'

Agapay's eyes shone as she nodded.

'Perhaps you can try some of the things out for them?' he continued, his blue eyes twinkling.

'Fab!' exclaimed Finn, while Vaz shrugged, pretending to be cool, though secretly he was just as intrigued and excited.

'Right! Off you go. Punch "Transport School Sirius" into the computer destination. You'll go through the nearest wormhole, so you'll only take a few seconds.' And the captain dematerialized.

There was a slight hiccup, for in his haste Finn typed TRAN-PORT SCOOL SIRIUS, missing letters out even though he knew perfectly well how to spell them. The computer said DESTINA-TION NOT RECOGNIZED and Finn retyped it, carefully this time.

They felt a whirr and a slight thud as they landed seconds later on a huge craft park, where extraordinary transports including rockets were lined up.

A Sirian with a big forehead, huge ears and welcoming smile awaited them. He was sitting cross-legged on a disc that hovered thirty centimetres above the ground. Magnetically attached to it were three similar discs, one pink, one navy and the third dark green.

'Hi, I'm Simindo,' the Sirian greeted them in impeccable English. 'Call me Si.'

'Hi Si,' they chorused, staring at him with big eyes.

He indicated that Agapay was to sit on the pink disc. 'It's been specially adjusted to your energy,' Si explained to her as she settled onto it.

The boys were clamouring to get on their discs but Si told them to wait, so they reluctantly watched as he showed them three buttons on the rim. 'This one is home and it will always take you there. In your case it will bring you back here to your spaceship. The second one is like an advanced satnav responding to voice commands. You must start by saying your name so that it recognizes you, then give it directions. Okay?'

They all nodded.

'And the third responds to everything else. It is also an emergency override. It will keep you safe by dropping to the ground or rising quickly.'

'How fast can it go?' Finn wanted to know.

'As fast as you need – but remember it is designed specifically for children to get to school or go short distances.'

'I'd love to go to school on this!' Agapay exclaimed and giggled. She pressed the middle knob and said clearly. 'Agapay. Forward.' The disc glided slowly and silently forward. 'Ooh!' she squealed. It felt so strange to be moving smoothly on a cushion of air.

'Go faster,' called Finn.

'And higher,' added Vaz. The girl sensibly ignored them and floated carefully away with Si beside her on his own disc. They glided round a stationary rocket and then over a low bridge that crossed a canal, watched by the impatient boys.

'Say "return home",' instructed Si carefully, 'and "Faster" – but only if you want to.'

Agapay did so cautiously and the disc turned gently and soared smoothly back to where the boys were standing.

'That was fab,' exclaimed the girl, who could see that the boys were raring to get onto their own discs. Finn's was the navy one and Vaz's the green one. She wondered what they would get up to.

No sooner had the boys sat on their discs than they were pressing the knobs, saying their names and giving instructions. To their disgust nothing happened.

'I've got you remotely locked,' Si told them. 'I need to give you lads some instructions first.'

Agapay put her hand to her mouth to hide her smile.

As soon as they had listened to him both boys simultaneously shouted their names and 'Fast' and then raced off. They were soon trying to fly over each other and rose as high as three metres, which was the highest the discs could go. They streaked towards the low bridge over the canal, competing to see who could get under it first. It looked as if they would collide but one of the craft automatically slowed down and slotted behind the other one so that they zoomed under it quite safely.

The boys even deliberately tried to crash into each other like bumper cars. They soon discovered that they couldn't quite touch, because the computer kept them apart. Later they learned that if they said 'Dock' the two discs would very gently connect to each other.

Agapay couldn't bear to watch them as she was sure they would crash, so she happily practised by herself at a reasonable speed on the other side of the craft park.

Suddenly all three found that their voice command was being ignored and the discs were returning all by themselves to where Si was watching. 'Remember these are intended for children,' he told them. 'And I put you on parental override to bring you back!'

The boys looked sheepish.

'Enough practice. We're going to the experimental laboratory now,' Si said to the children. Then he pressed the appropriate button, said, 'Disc 2, 3 and 4 dock to 1,' and immediately their transports linked easily together like four beads in a chain. 'To the Transport Lab please,' Si commanded and led the way.

'Do you say please to a computer?' Agapay asked in astonishment.

'You don't have to but advanced computers respond to emotions as well as commands so it is very wise to do so.'

'Oh!'

And with that Si set off at a cracking pace with the three children strung out behind him.

'Wow! Look there,' called out Finn, pointing at a group of people who were flying effortlessly through the air above them.

Si laughed. 'Oh they've got flypacks on.'

Agapay was round-eyed. 'What if they collide? Or if they fall out of the air?'

Si roared with laughter. 'That's impossible. The programmes wouldn't let that happen. They would simply avoid each other. You see, different types of transport travel in the different height bands and they are designed so that they can't touch each other within that wavelength or when they are passing through a different one.'

'I see,' said Agapay, nodding, taking this in carefully.

'Can we have a go with a flypack?' begged Finn.

'When we get to the lab!' the big man promised. He waved to some children who were whizzing along on discs playing catch. Agapay closed her eyes – she was sure one of the little boys was going to fall off.

'You need safety rails for the little ones,' she suggested. 'I've got two little brothers and they'd fall off that.'

'Oh yes. Good idea,' agreed Si and pressed the third knob to record the suggestion and transmit it to the laboratory supervisor.

THE TRANSPORT LAB

The Transport Lab turned out to be a pyramid-shaped building with transparent walls that looked like glass, but were apparently a special material that kept the temperature comfortable while letting in certain light spectrums.

The children soon found that the walls had another property – there was no door and Si led them straight through the 'glass' into the interior. It felt as if they were going through a cold draught. Inside there were about fifty beings of all ages, shapes and sizes in white coats, sitting at tables, intently working on their projects. Some looked up and smiled a welcome as the children floated in but most were too engrossed in what they were doing.

To his astonishment Finn recognized one as a boy who was in his class at school. 'Hey, that's Tweetie,' he said, pointing at a boy of his own age with big glasses, untidy mousy hair and a freckly face. The boy looked shocked to see him. He went pale and almost shrank as if he was trying to become invisible.

'What are you doing here, Tweetie Pie?' Finn called.

A strange thing happened. At school everyone laughed and joined in when the kids teased the boy with the big glasses. Now there was a surprised and rather cool silence. Finn felt embarrassed.

Agapay tried to help. 'What is your real name?' she asked the boy gently.

'R-richard,' he stammered.

Finn felt he had to explain. He half-laughed. 'Yeah, Dick is short for Richard, so at school we called him Dicky bird and now it's Tweet tweet or Tweetie Pie. It doesn't mean anything.' But everyone knew that it was meant unkindly. Agapay turned to Finn and said coldly, 'I never thought of you as a bully.'

Finn swallowed. He'd never considered it like that.

Si said quietly, 'In the future, when Richard grows up, he will be a famous scientist and inventor who will help the people on Earth a great deal. He is already learning a lot about spiritual technology and we think very highly of him.'

'Sorry,' responded Finn, feeling like a worm. He was usually a kind person and had always told himself it was just teasing, but he had seen the boy's reaction and felt ashamed. He glided on his disc to Richard's side, looking at the boy with new eyes. 'I'm sorry, Richard,' he said humbly. 'I'll never call you that again.'

The pale face reddened. 'That's all right,' Richard muttered.

'What are you doing and how do you get here? Do you come in a spaceship too?' Finn was curious.

'I come from Sirius – that is my soul does – and I come here most nights to learn in the tech schools,' Richard replied.

'In a spaceship like us?'

'No, I can fly in my spirit body. I sort of teleport with the angels.'

Vaz, Agapay and Si had joined Finn and now they too were floating on their discs beside Richard. 'Angels!' exclaimed the children together in astonishment.

'Angels,' repeated Si firmly. 'Look around you. Can you see the golden lights next to the scientists? They're dropping new ideas into their minds. Then they will guide them on how to make the inventions. The angels and scientists are preparing the technology for the Earth of the future so that things will be "invented" when the time is right.'

Finn frowned as he listened to Si. 'But—'

Si continued, ignoring him, 'Incidentally, that's why some inventions appear in different parts of the world at the same time.'

'Ah!' That had lit a light of understanding for Finn.

'You mean there really are angels?' asked Agapay.

'Of course. They are beings of light and are on a different wavelength from humans – one that most humans can't see. Most of you wouldn't do very well without your guardian angel helping you.'

The children were quiet for a moment. Then Richard pointed to a magnifying glass. 'Look. I am working on a battery that can hold a much greater charge than our current ones.' When Finn looked into it all he could see was a tiny golden ball a little bigger than a ball bearing.

Richard suddenly became animated. 'Have you seen people flying above the ground?'

The children nodded.

'They've got flypacks on. They are in the mini rucksacks they are wearing. They contain tiny battery-operated engines controlled by a computer. It propels them so they can move in a certain frequency band between three and six metres above the ground.'

'But those batteries must be so tiny!' exclaimed Finn. 'Are they the ones you are working on?'

Richard nodded modestly. 'The battery is charged by the sun and is a thousand times more powerful than anything on Earth right now. It's the size of a small nailhead and it has a five-kilometre range, which is rather limiting. I'm working on a more powerful one.'

'Wow!' The children were looking in awe at Richard. Then as one they turned and looked at Si. 'Please can we try the flypacks now?'

'We may have some adjustments to suggest that would help humans,' pleaded Finn and Si laughed. 'They are meant for adults but … Oh come on then. And you too, Richard. You've done enough for tonight and you'll have to go home soon. You've got school tomorrow.' He looked meaningfully at Finn, then added, 'Richard comes here during his sleep and if he remembers what happens he will think it is a dream. Don't tell him anything unless he asks. Right?'

Finn nodded.

Richard and Si helped the trio on with their mini backpacks and showed them how to set their destination so that the flypack would take them there automatically. They were also told they could change the instructions at any time, for the computer would respond to their thoughts.

'Let's go,' announced Richard, who looked like a different boy, confident and relaxed. Here he was in his element. He shot up into the air and called down, 'Follow me! Relax and you'll be fine.'

Somehow the children found themselves three metres above the ground. Richard grabbed Agapay's hand and they soared off. Strangely, she found that she loved it. 'I feel more in control than I did on the disc,' she shouted as the wind whipped back her long hair and tore out the rose petals, which showered round her. 'I kept feeling that I might fall off that but this is fab.'

Before long Richard showed her how to do a somersault in the air and she got the hang of it immediately. She just imagined herself flipping over and it happened.

Finn and Vaz were finding it much more difficult. They shot off in different directions. 'Keep your thoughts focused,' called Richard. The boys saw that Si was grinning at them but not unkindly. Nevertheless they both went beetroot-red, especially as Agapay had mastered it so easily. Richard raced up to them and grabbed their hands. With a little help they were soon flying everywhere confidently. 'Fantastic,' shouted Finn while Vaz screeched, 'Wheeeeee!!' as he vaulted over a tree, deliberately scattering small birds in all directions.

Richard told him reprovingly that people were expected to honour nature and animals and respect their right to their space.

'Sorry,' muttered Vaz but his eyes were alight with excitement. Gone was the cool, sulky boy who had got into the spacecraft.

Time seemed to rush by. They saw family-sized transports moving above their heads in the next waveband, then a couple of enormous transporters, the size of double-decker trains, flashed silently over them at a much higher level. It was eerie how they flew so quietly.

'You wanted human feedback, Si,' said Agapay seriously. She was always very conscientious, despite her unusual hair, which gave a hippy impression. 'I think it would be very useful if the flypacks could fit round the waist like a belt and that would mean people could carry things in a backpack, like shopping or even a baby!'

Si looked at her with a smile. 'Thanks Agapay. That's really helpful. I'll pass it on to the scientists who are working on it. We don't always think of things in a human way.' And Agapay flushed with pleasure.

The man turned to Richard and called, 'Time for you to go home now, Richard.'

The boy glanced at his watch and responded regretfully, 'You're right. I'm late already and I might be too tired to get up.'

He steered to the ground, waved goodbye and instantly vanished.

The following day Finn was early for school. He greeted his mates cheerily and even wondered if he had imagined his visit to Sirius. Then his glance caught Richard, who was skulking in the playground with his head down looking as if he dreaded anyone approaching him.

Finn walked up to him and saw a strange look come into the boy's eyes. 'I dreamed about you,' Richard stammered, then looked as if he could bite his tongue off. Admitting to a dream, let alone a dream about someone, was asking for trouble at school. But Finn responded, 'Hi Richard,' and sat down beside him. 'Tell me about your dream,' he said.

That was odd. Finn was one of the sportiest boys in the class and did not usually talk to nerds. And he'd called him Richard instead of Tweetie Pie. The boy smiled. It was as if he knew his life was going to change – and it did. From that day Finn quietly protected him and ensured that he was called Richard. The other kids soon followed suit. What would they say if they knew he was going to be a famous scientist one day! Finn glanced round the playground at some of the other children and wondered what they did in other dimensions. Was he the only one travelling to another world? Suddenly he looked at them all with new eyes and speculated on all sorts of possibilities.

CHAPTER 8

SPACE EDUCATION

The three children, Finn, Agapay and Vaz, were once more sitting in the spacecraft waiting for Captain Ambrose. The computer was programmed to take them to Sirius Education Department.

Vaz felt grumpy at the thought of it. 'School on Earth is boring,' he moaned. 'I bet it's the same on Sirius. All teachers want to do is cram your mind with useless information.'

The other two did not respond. Agapay was fiddling with her new hairstyle, purple plaits with gold lights running through them, and thinking about the delights of flying, while Finn could not wait for Captain Ambrose to arrive.

He wondered if he would see Richard this time. It was strange how they had become friends at school even though the boy could only remember that Finn had come into one of his dreams and did not even know that they had met on Sirius. He ran his hands through his short blond hair without knowing he was doing it. He always felt guilty when he thought how much happier Richard looked now that he wasn't being teased by the kids in the playground.

When the captain apported into the craft the trio had lots of questions to ask him.

'Will we be met by Si on discs?'

'Can we fly with the flypacks again?'

'Will we see Richard?'

'What is school like there?'

Captain Ambrose raised his hands to fend off the torrent of questions, though his bright blue eyes were twinkling with the hint of a smile. 'Okay guys. Here are the answers. Si will meet you but not on a flying disc – in a different kind of transport. You may have time to fly with the flypacks. Yes, you will see Richard.

About the Space School, remember we are working on spiritual technology for the future, so this visit will be about the technology to be used to teach children in years to come. I think you'll be amazed. And we know children learn best when they are relaxed and preferably having fun. So look forward to learning with fun and being creative.'

'Why do you always call it spiritual technology rather than just technology?' put in Agapay quickly.

'That's simple,' responded the spaceman. 'Spiritual technology uses natural materials like crystals and the power of the sun or waves and doesn't do any damage to the Earth or people. There's no waste products. And the high frequencies we use for telecommunications are not harmful to dolphins or bees – or humans for that matter.'

The children all nodded and thought how brilliant it would be when that came to Earth.

'Now it's time to activate your destination.' Captain Ambrose turned to the computer and commanded, 'Sirius Education Department.'

Without thinking Agapay added, 'Please.' Then she blushed and covered her mouth, thinking she might have been cheeky, but the captain said to her, 'You are right. Always better to ask properly!' And they all laughed.

In an instant they had landed on Sirius and were being greeted by Si's happy smiling face. 'Hi!' they all shouted, laughing and waving to him.

Si was standing beside a sleek, shining, bright red, oval-shaped transport, rather like a small spaceship. Finn and Vaz stared at it as if their eyes might pop out. Agapay's smile was as wide as a house. Si got into the front. 'Come on guys. What are you waiting for?'

The children leapt from their spacecraft and scrambled in. Finn sat beside Si while Vaz and Agapay were in the back. The first thing they noticed was that there were no seat belts. 'We don't need them. There are no accidents or sudden stops. Our advanced technology looks after everything,' Si explained.

He pressed a button and said, 'To the School please,' and the transport rose gently into the appropriate waveband where it soared silently as an eagle.

'You didn't say your name first,' commented Agapay, who always noticed these things.

'You're quite right,' replied Si. 'You say your name when you travel on the discs because they are individually tuned for each child so that the parents can take control if necessary. This one is for general use, so anyone can use it.'

Agapay nodded and sank back into the comfortable seat. Si continued. 'By the time Earth is ready for these, people will share things, so a family or group of friends will call a transport from a general pool when they need it and it will be sent to them by remote control.'

'Oh cool!' exclaimed Finn and then added predictably, 'How fast can it go?'

Si smiled and said into the speaker. 'Maximum speed please.' They scarcely felt the acceleration but the speedometer rose to 500 km an hour.

Seconds later the computer announced, 'Approaching destination.' The transport decelerated and landed as softly as a feather on a calm day in front of a multicoloured pyramid. A sign announced EDUCATION DEPARTMENT.

'We're here,' remarked Si unnecessarily.

Vaz sighed. He had loved the flight and did not want it to end.

'Why another pyramid?' queried Agapay, insatiable for knowledge as usual, tugging her purple plaits. 'The Transport School was a pyramid too.'

'That's because a pyramid is a sacred geometrical shape that can alter vibrations and help bring things into balance. There are lots of shapes and they all have a different effect.'

'How?' Agapay wanted to know.

'Imagine if you put a wooden triangle in a river. The water would flow round it in a certain way. And it would move round a square or a circle differently. The technology of your future works with currents of energy.'

Finn muttered, 'Sounds a bit like maths to me,' and switched off, but Vaz was intrigued. 'So oblongs and stars and figures of eight for instance all affect things differently?'

'Yup,' agreed Si. 'You've got it. They change the flow. Look! Here comes Richard to meet us.'

The three children shouted, 'Hi!' to Richard.

'Great to see you,' he called back and plunged straight into telling them about his work before they had even got out of the transport.

'We don't think it is appropriate to stuff children with other people's knowledge,' he explained, 'So we're developing learning by experience. This means bringing virtual reality into the classroom. This is the way children on Earth will be taught soon. '

'How does that work?' asked Finn in amazement.

Richard laughed. He was twirling his glasses in his hands and looked much older and less nerdy without them on, despite the dressing gown he was wearing with a donkey on it, clearly bought by an aunt or a gran. 'Let's go in and find out,' he suggested. They followed him into a room with a giant screen at the far end.

'What would you like to learn about?' asked Richard. They all looked blank until Finn suddenly said, 'Coral reefs. I'm going on holiday with my parents next month.'

'Lucky you,' muttered Vaz but Finn did not even hear. He was excitedly accepting a pencil-sized control-wand from Richard, who asked the others if they wanted to experience and learn about coral reefs too. When they nodded, he handed a wand to each of them.

'Now remember,' he advised them. 'This is virtual so there is no danger here. Nothing can harm you. If you want to come out of the experience just press the red button or say "Out!" If you want to know something, think the question and it will be answered by an expert.'

'Cool,' exclaimed Finn, who was jumping with anticipation.

'I think I'll come with you,' said Si and they all felt relieved. 'I am an expert on marine life,' he added in a matter-of-fact tone.

Richard continued. 'If you want to share the questions and answers with the others you press the green button, otherwise you have your own personal experience. If you would like others to join you say their names or think about them and they will come into your new reality. Oh, and if you leave virtual reality at any time and then you want to go back in, press blue.'

Finn could not believe what he was hearing. 'I want to meet a shark,' he announced with bravado.

Agapay raised her eyes and said, 'Boys!' but no one heard her. Vaz was thinking about a pirate ship full of treasure but that was only a passing thought and did not have any impact on what they were to experience.

'Have you snorkelled before?' asked Richard. The boys had but Agapay had not, so Richard told her not to worry, Si would help her.

Bemused but excited, they waited for Richard to bring up the right programme.

Suddenly Finn realized he was wearing a mask and flippers and was looking down at a beautiful coral reef, alive with colourful darting fish and fronds of seaweed. He smelled the salty freshness of the ocean as he dived into the cool aquamarine water and found himself in the middle of a shoal of zebra fish. An angelfish brushed past his ear. He could see Richard and Vaz swimming nearby, followed by Agapay with Si, who was helping her to coordinate her flippers and manage her mask.

They were all wearing snugly fitting swimsuits, like comfortable wetsuits made from some unknown material. Finn realized he was not at all cold.

It felt very real and he found himself thinking uneasily that there really might be sharks in the water. Immediately Si responded in a reassuring voice. 'There are sharks here but they will not harm you.' Then he continued to tell him all about different kinds of sharks. Moments later Si advised Finn to look to the right and he would see one. Ooh, it was big! Finn gulped and told himself it was virtual, but it certainly felt as if it was real.

Si was explaining that sharks' teeth move forward on a kind of conveyor belt, so that there were always strong ones at the front, when, to Finn's horror, the shark turned and swam straight towards him. It opened its jaws wide so that Finn could see the rows of terrible teeth. His heart seemed to stop beating for a moment in sheer terror.

Sweating, he automatically pressed the red button and came out of the experience. One thing was certain – he would never forget about sharks' teeth!

He found himself in the virtual-reality room looking at a flat screen of a coral reef with Si, Agapay and Vaz snorkelling over it. They seemed to be having a wonderful time floating across a deep wide chasm with white sand below and reefs on either side.

They were swimming with a pod of dolphins. He could see that Agapay wanted to reach out and touch one that was very close, but then she obviously realized she must not touch a wild creature and drew her hand back in again.

A female dolphin had a tiny baby beside her and it looked very cute as it glided near its mother.

Then one dolphin flapped the water with its flipper and Si told them that meant there was danger about. Immediately the two children looked round in concern but the man pointed out that there was a shark swimming away from the reef and they sighed with relief. Finn recognized it too!

He pressed the blue button and re-entered the cool green ocean world. Instantly he found two dolphins beside him and together they surged to the surface in a fizz of bubbles. He felt alive and exhilarated. As they played with the dolphins Si explained that they were warm-blooded like humans and gave birth to live babies. He pointed to the blowholes on the top of their heads. 'They breathe through their blowholes,' he explained. 'If they get water in there they will drown, so they blow any water out and close the hole when they dive underwater.

'Oh!' exclaimed Agapay, very interested. 'How do they sleep?'

'Good question,' said Si, beaming. 'Because they have to keep breathing they shut down half of their brain when they sleep. So they catnap just below the surface of the water and come up to breathe.'

'What about their sonar?' Vaz wanted to know; he could hear it clicking.

'It lets them tell whether or not the water in front of them is clear so that they can find their way. Oh look! They want to put on a display for you,' Si told them. And they watched happily as two dolphins swam together, joyfully leaping, swimming in synchrony and twisting.

'Time to finish, I think,' announced Si at last. 'You have other things to experience.'

Reluctantly they pressed their red buttons and found themselves in the room in front of the flat screen. Finn kept expecting a fish to float past him but no. He was back in ordinary reality.

'Wow!' commented Agapay. 'I absolutely loved those dolphins. I want to find out more.'

'That's the idea!' nodded Si.

'I … didn't like the shark,' muttered Finn, but so quietly that the others could not hear him.

'What else can you learn about in virtual reality? How about history?' Agapay wanted to know.

'History is especially interesting to learn about in this way,' enthused Richard. 'Originally it was written by the side that won the wars and that distorts what really happened. But in our advanced computers the truth is recorded so children can see all the perspectives and can know what was really going on at that time.'

'That's wild!' said Finn.

'How about going into the life of Henry VIII? Then you'll get a feel for what really happened to his six wives.' Richard was clearly fired up.

But at the same instant Finn and Agapay thought about the two wives who were beheaded. 'Er, no thanks!' they responded simultaneously.

'What about chemistry then?' Richard offered. 'You can mix the chemicals and see what happens but if it explodes you won't get hurt.'

'Great idea!' Vaz, who liked chemistry, was suddenly alert and excited.

But at that moment Si's watch, which was really an advanced computer, buzzed and, seemingly floating in the air above it, an invitation appeared to listen to Lord Hilarion talk in the Grand Pyramid.

'I'm going,' said Richard instantly. 'I've always wanted to hear him.'

'Who is he?' demanded Agapay.

'Who wants to listen to a lord?' commented Vaz disdainfully.

'You've never heard of Hilarion?' exclaimed Richard, looking aghast. Si responded calmly. 'Hilarion is a Lord of Light, a title which he had to earn. He is in charge of bringing in the new spiritual science and technology to Earth.'

Vaz looked bemused and for once didn't know what to say.

'Come on!' urged Richard. 'This should be good!'

CHAPTER 9

LORD HILARION AND THE SPIDER

'So what's this Lord Hilarion going to be talking about?' queried Agapay.

'Lessons from spiders!' responded Si, glancing at his super-screen. 'And I bet they have lots to teach us.'

The children made faces but jumped up all the same to follow him. The Sirian had long legs and they had to run to keep up.

The Grand Pyramid lived up to its name. It was vast. Inside there were tiers of comfortable seats and already hundreds of interested people and beings of various shapes and sizes had arrived. The five of them sat down somewhere in the middle, next to a woman with an elongated head who evidently came from another universe and a being that looked rather like a horse. All at once Agapay let out a shriek. 'Look, that girl's in my school! She's in the year above me. What's she doing here, Si? Does she do what we do?'

Si glanced at the screen above his watch. It was showing a picture of the girl and some written information about her. He shook his head. 'No, she's training to be an intergalactic ambassador and she does most of her work in her sleep at night.'

The girl became aware of Agapay staring at her and waved. She did not seem in the least bit surprised to see the younger girl.

It was Vaz's turn to be startled. 'That's my uncle,' he whispered, pointing to a thin man sitting alone on the front row, who glanced up at the boy in surprise. 'And, over there's my physics teacher.' Vaz sat back looking quite pale. 'Will my uncle remember seeing me here when we're back on Earth? He doesn't believe in UFOs and weird things. I keep my mouth shut when he comes round.'

Si reassured him that his uncle would almost certainly forget that he'd seen him.

'What's he doing here anyway?' demanded Vaz, as if he was the only one who had a right to be there! 'He works for the tax office!'

Si smiled at the boy's annoyance. 'Your uncle is learning certain lessons on Earth in the day and in his sleep his spirit is a teacher on another planet. He is here tonight, just as you are, to learn.'

Vaz was silent with shock, which was just as well for at that moment a ripple of excitement ran through the pyramid and a tall slim man surrounded by a shimmering orange and blue light appeared on the platform in the centre. It was Lord Hilarion. There was silence as the majestic figure held up a hand and orange light beamed from it, connecting with everyone in the great hall.

Finn felt a thud in his third eye in the centre of his forehead and knew some sort of connection had been made. He glanced at Agapay and Vaz and knew that they had had the same experience. While Hilarion talked, different coloured lights moved and pulsed round him. At the same time his aura seemed to reach out and touch some of the beings in the audience, who were all watching him intently. In other cases it pulled something from them and often they would cry as if in relief. It was mesmerizing to watch.

Suddenly Finn realized that a screen had appeared in front of him. As in the virtual-reality room, the picture was 3D and instantly he was actually in the scene, standing by a spider's web while Hilarion's deep voice talked about the insects, which, he told them, came from a different universe in order to teach beings in this one.

That came as a surprise to the children, who murmured in astonishment.

They watched the spider weaving its web according to the principles of sacred geometry. 'When anyone uses sacred geometric shapes for anything at all, the flow is so beautiful that the angels sing over them,' Hilarion explained, 'and when that happens miracles can take place.'

He continued, 'If humans or indeed any of you were constructing something like this web against gravity, you would tend to think of all the reasons it could not be done. You would focus on the difficulties and think you'd never be good enough to do it. Most of you would doubt that it was even possible. This is why you make

certain things impossible for yourselves.' People were nodding to themselves in agreement.

They watched spellbound as the spider looped its silken thread into a simple pattern. It never paused but moved slowly and determinedly upward towards completion. A fly zoomed noisily past

Finn straight into the web. The spider leapt suddenly and Finn could not help jumping too. He flushed. Then he noticed that lots of others had reacted in the same way. 3D-computers were sometimes a bit too realistic, he decided.

Hilarion smiled as the spider stood triumphantly in the centre of its wonderful and perfect complex web. 'Now this wise creature,' he continued, 'simply holds his vision of the final outcome. As you know, when this happens the energy of the universe supports the vision and it has to happen. This little arachnid is teaching us all about sacred geometry, faith and tenacity. Even if I broke the web it would remake it. It knows that everything is possible and has just demonstrated it to us beautifully.'

Everyone nodded while Agapay murmured to Vaz, 'What's an arachnid?'

'An eight-legged insect,' he murmured out of the side of his mouth.

'When you are working on spiritual technology remember this spider. Today's lesson is – hold your vision and the forces of the universe will make sure it will come about. Thank you for coming.'

And with that the Master's body shimmered and faded slowly out of sight. Finn, Agapay and Vaz stared at the empty space. Singly or in groups, most of the beings apported from their seats to their destinations, but a number left the pyramid on their own two feet. The children walked behind Si and Richard.

'So,' said Agapay when they were outside again, 'Children in the future will learn by virtual-reality experiences and by lectures during which they watch the demonstration on their own screens.'

'And every student will have their own watch-link, into which will be downloaded the lessons specifically for them. There will be lots of individual tuition but all learning will be fun.'

'Will there be books, I wonder?' mused Finn.

Si responded that there would always be books, for there is a kind of magic about the feel of a book and the turning page that simply isn't there with electronic versions. 'But electronic books will be much more sophisticated. Birds will sing the dawn chorus if you read about the sunrise. You will smell the freshness of the countryside as it is being described. If you identify with a character you will feel not just his feelings, but his health and happiness or his illness.' He saw Agapay's horrified look but it was Finn who put it into words. 'You mean if the hero breaks a leg I'll feel as if mine is broken too!'

'You can always turn that option off,' murmured Si. 'Time is marching on, I'm afraid, so we have to move on too.'

They all groaned.

'There is one more thing.' Richard was jumping up and down in his desire to share his knowledge. 'Can we show them the IDAS and the tele-link and can they come back for the fun math programme and—'

'What are IDAS?' demanded Finn and Agapay at the same moment.

Si laughed. 'They are inter-dimensional audio specs but we're done for today. And kids, on your next visit you'll be exploring how the technology of the future will be used in hospitals for healing people.'

'Oh yes!' exclaimed Agapay, who wanted her mum to get better. 'I'd love to see that! Do you think it could help my mum?'

'Patience!' replied Si annoyingly, smiling at her eagerness. 'Let's get you back to your spacecraft now.' Seconds later they watched their transport float down the road towards them.

The big man turned to Richard. 'And here's some energy to get you back home in your spirit body.' He sent a golden ball of light to the boy, who exploded like a firework and disappeared.

CHAPTER 10

THE PLOT TO TAKE OVER PLANET EARTH

One night, Finn, Vaz and Agapay found themselves all of a sudden in a vast spacecraft, bigger than ten ocean-going liners. It was full of lights and humming sounds, computers and silent people.

'We're in the mothership,' gasped Finn, looking round in awe.

'What's that?' whispered Agapay.

'The main spaceship. It's a docking station and all the commands come from here! Captain Ambrose told me about it.'

'Wow,' uttered Vaz, itching to touch some of the weird-looking gadgets.

'Cool,' murmured Agapay.

At that moment Captain Ambrose appeared in front of them looking very worried. The children eyed him anxiously. Whatever could be the matter?

'Hi guys,' he greeted them soberly.

'Hello Captain,' they chanted in unison, then waited apprehensively for him to communicate what was wrong.

'I've got a job for you. On an asteroid in another universe an evil being has created giant locusts. If they reach us they could destroy all the crops on our planet.'

The children were horrified.

But Finn was puzzled too. 'How can they get here through space?'

'In space capsules designed to disintegrate when the temperature is right so that the locusts will be ready to hatch.'

'But how can they get through the defences round the planet?' Finn persisted.

Captain Ambrose sighed. 'We can no longer afford to patrol

all the entry portals. They will easily slip through where there is no security.'

Agapay asked, 'Why would they want to do that to us?'

'They want our minerals and metals, like gold, uranium, iron, copper and plutonium. If the locusts have eaten everything and all the people and animals starve to death, they will have free access to our riches. They just have to wait.'

'Oh.'

'So what do you want us to do?' queried Vaz after a silence.

Captain Ambrose sounded very efficient. 'Go to Asteroid Evlop and discover their plan. Stop them if you can. Find their proposed entry points if you can't so that we can defend them.' He paused. 'And …'

The children waited expectantly. He continued. 'We don't know who is behind this plan. Find out who it is if you can.'

The trio nodded numbly. Each was thinking, 'An arch-villain, a plot to take over Earth.' It couldn't get much worse.

But they had no time to respond. In a flash they found themselves wearing their spacesuits and hurtling into their spacecraft. Night, the spacecraft cat, was waiting. 'I'll catch all the locusts and eat them,' he growled darkly to Agapay, who conveyed this to the others. They did not ask how he knew about them – that cat had his own methods of finding things out.

'Let's go,' declared Finn hurriedly, typing DESTINATION ASTEROID EVLOP into the computer.

They heard the usual whirr and felt a thump as they landed nanoseconds later. All three ran to look out of the window but they could only see strange octagonal-shaped buildings. There were no living creatures to be seen. It was rather spooky.

'Better explore,' announced Finn.

'Please make us invisible first,' implored Agapay, who had a horrid feeling in the pit of her stomach.

'Sure,' replied Vaz, who could feel the tension.

Night uttered a short meow and Agapay looked at him sharply. She listened intently as he continued. 'Oh,' she responded, 'Thank you Night.' She turned to Finn and Vaz. 'He says we must make the spacecraft invisible too.'

'What about him? Shall I make him disappear too?'

Agapay and Night both shook their heads. 'He says the Evil One is afraid of cats. Besides, if he stays with the craft we'll know where it is.' She paused and giggled. 'He says he'll eat any locusts he catches.' Night looked fierce.

The boys smiled, which helped to ease the tension.

They all held hands so that they wouldn't lose each other and a few seconds later their craft became invisible too. It felt a bit scary but they felt better when they saw Night sitting defiantly on a rock nearby.

The children crept towards the octagonal buildings hoping that the arrival of the spacecraft had not been noticed, but seconds later a creature emerged from the building. He had a huge square head with big square eyes, tiny ears, mouth, nose, body and legs and short arms with ten fingers on each hand.

The creature clicked the ten fingers of his left hand and a giant ant appeared. It flattened itself in front of the square being who stepped onto it. The ant then rose up and carried the Evil One rapidly towards Night, who was still sitting by the invisible spacecraft.

'Quick. It's our chance to look inside the buildings,' whispered Finn and the trio set off towards them. They slowed down as they approached the main entrance. What would they find inside?

They were shocked by what they saw. Conveyor belts stretched the length of the huge building carrying huge locust eggs to crates where they were being packed by machinery into space capsules.

A dozen giant ants, with huge control boxes strapped to their backs, were supervising the operation. The children watched as the full capsule closed and was stacked with hundreds of thousands of similar ones.

Suddenly the control boxes crackled and they heard an angry voice booming. Agapay could understand and she listened intently, then gave a gasp. The giant ants heard it and swivelled suspiciously towards the sound. The children stood silently holding their breaths until the ants turned and raced out of the building.

'What did it say?' whispered Finn and Vaz together.

Agapay kept her voice low. 'He said, "Xander here," so that must be his name. Then he told them that the defences were breached and there was a strange alien among them.'

'That must be the cat,' said Finn.

'Yes. But he said they must bring the attack forward. All systems go for the launch tonight.'

The boys were horrified. 'We've got to find out what entry portals they are aiming at,' announced Finn decisively. 'That's the best thing we can do.'

'Let's scatter and see what we can find. Meet up again by Night, next to the spacecraft,' suggested Vaz. The others agreed and they spread out in the honeycomb of buildings.

It was Finn who found the command office first. On the wall was a chart of Earth. The main portals were indicated with a cross. Finn recognized Stonehenge in the UK, Machu Picchu in Peru and Uluru in Australia but there were lots of others as well. Then he saw that there were ten red circles marked. All of a sudden he knew this was what he was looking for. This was where the capsules could breach the defences of Earth. He couldn't possibly remember them all, so quickly he took the map off the wall and rolled it up. To his relief it became invisible as soon as he took hold of it. Now back to Night and the spacecraft!

Vaz was not so fortunate in his search. He opened a closed door and was hit by a surge of insects. They flew into his hair, his face, his clothes and he yelled as he battled to close the door on them. At last he succeeded but there were locusts everywhere. 'I'm a Celebrity, Get Me Out of Here,' he muttered to himself and vowed he'd never laugh at the contestants on that show again.

Suddenly there was an unearthly yowl as Night sprang into the midst of the locusts, catching some and biting their heads off with relish. Vaz sat on the floor and watched.

Agapay was even unluckier. In her hurry to find out where the capsules would be propelled through Earth's defences she ran as fast as she could – and tripped. She fell heavily, crying out as she hit the floor, and the shock caused the invisibility spell to lift. Now she was in full view of Xander and the giant ants, who were on their way back in to the honeycomb building, looking for the cat. The Evil One roared and she screamed.

Finn couldn't find the spacecraft now that Night had left and gone to hunt locusts, so he sat on a rock and called Captain Ambrose on his space link. 'The name of the Being is Xander,' he informed him.

He heard the captain's grim response. 'We know him well, very well. Get out as soon as you can.'

Finn's heart sank and he felt rather sick but he said, 'I know where the attacks will come. I've found the map.' He unfolded it as he spoke and his voice shook slightly as he described the positions of the ten entry portals shown on the map.

It was then that he heard Agapay's scream. Dropping the map, he ran towards the building.

By the time he reached it Agapay was sitting up surrounded by the killer ants and Xander was pointing at her, uttering screams of rage.

Finn's hands flew to his mouth. He wished he knew where Vaz was. What could he do? 'I wish our dragons were here,' he thought.

No sooner had the thought gone through his head than there was a thunderous roar and the three huge orange dragons burst into the room.

'You called us!' Flame shouted. Because the dragons can see through the dimensions he knew where invisible Finn was standing.

'No, I didn't.'

'You thought of us. That was enough.'

'Oh,' said Finn with a sigh of understanding and relief.

In a flash the dragons started spewing out flames, which terrified the ants and made them run away. Before they could stop him Xander dashed across to the far wall and pressed a button. 'Too late,' he jeered. 'You can't stop me.'

There was an eerie noise as a hundred thousand silver capsules launched themselves towards Earth.

Xander screamed as a dragon sent a jet of flame towards him and singed his hair.

Finn and Vaz suddenly became visible. Finn turned to Xander. 'No, it is you who is too late,' he said quietly but jubilantly. 'We know which portals they are aimed at.' He hoped fervently that Captain Ambrose had managed to seal them.

Xander howled. At the very same moment Night squealed to Agapay. 'Get out of here fast.' The girl picked up the cat and instantly the three dragons swooped towards their charges and scooped them up.

In a flash they were inside the spacecraft and pressing the home button.

All at once they realized why Xander had screamed. As they hurtled away they saw that the capsules had bounced off the closed portals and were returning to their point of origin. Xander was about to be deluged with super-locusts.

Night, the cat, looked as though he was grinning as he spoke to Agapay. 'That's karma for you,' she translated for them.

'What does that mean?' Finn asked.

'What you give out always comes back to you – but not usually as quickly as that,' Agapay translated for Night. 'Well done us.'

'Yes. Well done us,' the boys echoed as their craft landed safely back on Earth.

CHAPTER 11

A Second Chance

Finn was feeling really tired after playing football most of the day, so he groaned when he felt the familiar sensation of being pulled out of bed and through his bedroom wall into the spacecraft. But as soon as he saw Vaz and Agapay (with purple bows in her hair) he started to buzz with anticipation.

Captain Ambrose smiled a greeting but then a familiar solemn expression settled over his face – oh no, that meant trouble. The space captain explained that he had been keeping an eye on Xander, the wicked square-headed being who had enslaved the huge ants and tried to attack Earth by bombarding it with rockets filled with monster-sized locust eggs ready to hatch.

'And we blocked the portals so they bounced right back to his asteroid,' crowed Finn, who was very pleased with his part in foiling that plot.

'So he got his karma back,' pointed out Agapay gleefully.

'Let me tell you what has happened,' said the captain before the children could continue. 'Locusts have eaten everything on Asteroid Evlop. It has been stripped bare. Xander shut himself away in his factory and now he has started to realize the enormity of what he has done. Something has changed in him – he has set the ants free and apologized. Now they are freely eating the eggs laid by the locusts that hatched. But it is too late to save the asteroid and the Intergalactic Council wants to help the ants and Xander.'

Agapay frowned. 'Help him!' she exclaimed. 'But surely he must pay karma for what he tried to do.'

'He should be punished,' agreed Vaz.

Captain Ambrose listened patiently to all of them, then spoke quietly. 'You are right about karma but it is not designed as punishment. It also offers an opportunity to learn lessons. Xander has shown remorse and so the universe will offer him a second chance. Doesn't that feel right to you?'

The children all nodded reluctantly, each secretly hoping they'd get a second chance if they did something wrong.

'So,' continued the captain. 'He needs the opportunity to help others. If he does so, we will know he has learned and changed.'

This time all three children agreed readily. 'Where do we come into it?' asked Vaz.

'Two things,' the spaceman replied. 'First we want you to go to Asteroid Evlop and see how Xander reacts to you.'

The children looked at each other nervously until Vaz said, 'I suppose I can make us invisible if there's trouble.'

'Or I could construct a wall between us,' added Finn, not to be outdone.

Agapay thought to herself that inter-species communication was always the best way. She met the captain's eyes and was sure he agreed.

'And secondly I'd like your ideas from a human perspective about where we can take Xander to give him a second chance.' The children were silent, deep in thought.

'Take him to the land of one-eyed black panthers,' growled Vaz, 'and see how he gets on there.'

Agapay was annoyed with him. 'Vaz! This is about helping others, not punishment. Don't you ever listen?' she said sharply.

Vaz gave her a dirty look. 'I was joking,' he protested, which they all knew was a lie.

Finn was thinking about the tiny red-haired boy and all the people who had escaped down the slide from the asteroid threatened by the super-volcano. How were they getting on? Were they coping? Could Xander somehow help them?

He mentioned this tentatively and the captain's eyes glowed a deep, extraordinary blue.

'Oh yes!' exclaimed Agapay. 'Maybe he'd have some ideas to help them – and they are such lovely beings. That would be brilliant.'

Vaz glowered. He still felt angry with Agapay. She returned his angry stare with a cold look. It was the first time any of them had had harsh words and everyone felt uncomfortable.

The captain frowned slightly at this negativity before he responded to Finn's question and Agapay's enthusiasm. 'You're right. I believe the beings there are struggling. They are trying to build homes and get their moss to grow but it has not been easy for them. It is much windier there and there is less water. Also,' he added, 'they have lots of heart but little brains.'

'And Xander has lots of brains but little heart,' finished Agapay. The captain nodded.

They were given detailed instructions from the captain about transporting the ants home to Sirius, where they came from, and warned to take no risks with Xander.

'And work together,' he reminded them with a slightly troubled expression as he shut the door of the spacecraft. In seconds they were passing through a wormhole and had landed on the asteroid.

What a scene of devastation met their eyes! The land was laid bare. Half-dead, starving locusts were fluttering about, while their newly laid eggs were being devoured by the huge ants that had been set free.

The door of the factory opened and Xander appeared, looking square and formidable. 'Shall I make us invisible?' offered Vaz but Agapay shook her head. 'Not yet, thank you,' she responded in a tight voice that indicated she was still annoyed. Vaz shrugged and, without asking, made Finn and then himself disappear. Agapay, in front of them, didn't realize this and walked towards Xander.

Xander saw a nine-year-old girl with bright orange bows in her hair approaching him. She was vaguely familiar. Suddenly he remembered. 'It was you!' he bellowed angrily. 'You and your friends caused this havoc.'

Agapay stood still. Vaz would make her invisible if Xander came closer. She had forgotten that their gifts only operated if they cooperated – and that meant being friends. Her heart was thumping as Xander rushed towards her. So was Vaz's as he realized his gift was not working.

The girl called to Xander that she wanted to speak to him. He snarled back that he had a lot to say to her too. He grabbed her arm in a vice-like grip and marched her off. She looked terrified.

Vaz was distraught. He had put Agapay in danger by his anger. He rushed after them with Finn in hot pursuit and they slipped through the door behind Agapay, just before Xander slammed it shut.

Agapay breathed deeply. She wished Finn and Vaz were with her – or, if they already were, that she could see them. She was so scared but determined to be brave. She spoke in Xander's language. 'I'm so sorry about what's happened to your home.'

A strange thing happened. Xander peered into her face as if he could hardly believe his ears. Then he let her go. He threw himself onto a crate and put his head in his hands. 'I'm sorry, I'm sorry, I'm sorry,' he whispered. 'I've been so wicked and I vowed I'd change but when I saw you the memory of what I lost overcame me. I hope I didn't hurt you.'

The girl looked at her bruised arm and said nothing. Xander and Vaz looked at her arm too. Suddenly Vaz decided to man up and make himself visible. Xander looked shocked when he appeared but this time he was not angry.

Agapay threw her arms round Vaz as he murmured, 'I'm sorry. I'm so sorry.' She knew what he meant and smiled, understanding. 'We all make mistakes, Vaz. I was wrong too.'

'So you'll give me a second chance?'

'Of course.'

The invisible Finn commented, 'Everyone deserves a second chance if they are sorry.'

Xander looked round for the disembodied voice but relaxed when Vaz and Agapay chuckled. When Finn appeared they all sat down and Agapay put to Xander the plan to take him to the place where he could help the little red-haired beings. At first he was reluctant. It was as if he did not feel worthy but as they discussed the plight of the beings he gradually became more enthusiastic. 'I could help them build an aqueduct to take the water where it is needed. And I could mechanize the gathering of moss and teach them all sorts of things.'

The children looked at Xander. His square head and square eyes had become rounder. How strange!

'So you want to go to that asteroid?' asked Finn. Agapay translated.

'Yes please – and thank you for the chance,' Xander responded. His smile and his gestures meant that Agapay did not need to translate this for the boys to understand it.

They called the ants and explained. The insects followed them joyfully to the spacecraft. Xander was amazed by everything. Finn sent a message to the red-haired leader to announce they would be arriving with a special visitor and explained that they must first go to Sirius.

Captain Ambrose had told them beforehand that ants come from Sirius and that they teach sacred geometry and other things wherever they go. They must programme the computer to take them via an inter-dimensional portal to a docking station outside the star cluster, where the ants would be transferred to another craft. Seconds later there was a whirring sensation, followed by deep silence, then a slight thud.

'We've docked,' announced Agapay unnecessarily.

The ants prepared to transfer to the craft from Sirius. They moved in single file between the two vehicles through a portalizer. As they did so they expanded into their true bodies, becoming tall golden, glowing beings.

'Wow!' murmured Vaz. 'The captain said ants were really incredible light beings and now I've seen it for myself.'

Xander was staring with his mouth open as if he could not believe what he had seen. 'I want to be like them,' he mouthed at last and Agapay gave him a hug, which embarrassed him. He was growing visibly taller, softer and rounder.

'Now to visit your new home,' said Finn, reprogramming the computer. 'They've received the message to say we are coming with a special visitor.' He smiled at Xander, who looked almost bashful.

When they landed they could see that everyone had come out to greet them. The little red-haired boy was holding a banner proclaiming, 'Krowpindo oo rogdip,' which Agapay said meant, 'Welcome friends and stranger too.' They noticed that Xander's pale face had flushed pink with pleasure.

As soon as the little boy saw Finn he ran towards him with his arms outstretched. Finn picked him up and twirled him round until he screamed with delight. Other children were running up to them and demanding to be twirled. They were rather shy of Xander but when he sat down the red-haired boy's elder sister climbed onto his knee. He looked overwhelmed with pleasure.

The leader announced that they had prepared a house for Xander. They could all tell that a family had moved out in order that he could have the space and that the house they had moved into was crammed. Xander gently placed the child on the ground. He stood and said softly, 'Thank you so much but a family needs that home. I am happy with a single hut.' He was becoming rounder by the minute.

The mother of the red-haired boy spoke up. 'We have a spare room. You are welcome to live with us.'

Unexpectedly, tears ran down Xander's cheeks. 'I've never been wanted before,' he murmured.

Xander was brimming with ideas to help the community and he had started to pick up their language already. He chatted briefly with the leader, though Agapay had to translate for him.

Then the mother and her two red-haired infants led Xander to his new home. The children watched them walk away. Xander's head was almost round now.

Finn, Agapay and Vaz declined kind offers of hospitality and boarded their craft.

'He deserved his second chance,' mused Vaz humbly.

'I think everyone deserves a second chance,' said Agapay, smiling at him. 'Including me.'

'Hear, hear,' agreed Finn, relieved that they were all friends again.

CHAPTER 12

FLYING DISCS ON EARTH?

Finn was in his bedroom thinking about travelling on the discs. Not only had it been great fun but he could just imagine the faces of all his friends if he arrived at school on one. He laughed out loud at the thought of it and stuffed his hand in his mouth in case his older brother, Blake, who was meant to be looking after him while his parents were out shopping, came to investigate.

Finn remembered when Captain Ambrose had first visited him and given him and the other children a gift. Finn grinned as he looked wryly at the strangely shaped three-legged china cow on the shelf in his bedroom that had been his first attempt to use his gift – the ability to build things from thin air, using just his imagination. He thought about Agapay's gift; she could communicate with all species. This had proved immensely helpful when they had met animals and all sorts of weird beings from all over the universes. Vaz could render himself and others invisible, and that had saved their lives a few times.

Now Finn wondered if he could use his gift to manifest a disc. He sat on his bed and focused on the feel of the special material and the round shape. Before long a large blue object, like a giant frisbee, appeared at his feet and he turned it over and sat on it. That was the easy bit. How could he possibly create the disc's miniature computer? Frustratingly but not surprisingly, even when he tried to imagine it nothing happened.

He slipped downstairs to find his mother's quartz crystal, hoping he could make it power up the disc. He sneaked it up to his room under his jumper. He certainly did not want his brother asking any questions.

Placing the quartz crystal on the disc, he sat cross-legged on it and focused on it rising up. Nothing happened! He spent an exasperating hour trying everything he could think of. Then an idea struck him. He would phone Richard!

He knew it was crazy really – Richard did not remember anything about their space travels – but Finn was so driven by the thought of creating a flying disc that he did not care.

He grabbed the phone from the kitchen and took it up to his room. To his delight Richard answered. He sounded more than a little surprised to hear Finn's voice but said he was sure his mother would not mind him coming over. Finn did not quite remember to mention that his parents were out!

Half an hour later Richard's mother dropped him off outside the gate and told him she would pick him up when he phoned for a lift.

For the next hour the boys remained closeted in Finn's room while he explained to his amazed and slightly sceptical friend that he was sure they could make the disc rise by the use of crystal power. He remembered Si's warning and did not dare tell Richard that he travelled to Sirius at night and invented spiritual technology. But as they talked the boy started to remember his experiences, rather like a dream that's there but will not quite surface. He got very frustrated as he tried to catch memories that just slipped away. However, he wanted to please his new friend, so if Finn thought he could create a computer programme and battery to enable a disc to fly, Richard would go along with it. Anyway, it was rather exciting.

Finn's house was one of a row perched on a hilltop. Behind it was a belt of trees; then a grassy slope ran down to a minor road. What better place to practise flying! They crept downstairs, carefully carrying the large round disc. As they went out of the back door Finn shouted to his brother that he was going to play on the hill and then they ran as fast as they could so that he could not ask any questions.

There was a light grey mist outside. It was dull without actually drizzling, and luckily there was no one about.

They tried sitting on the disc and willing it to rise. That didn't work. They took it in turns to hold the crystal and imagine the disc flying. That didn't work either. For a time they slid down the grassy slope on it. That was fun but not quite what Finn had in mind and he felt impatient.

Suddenly Richard put his hand in his pocket and felt something tiny in it. He pulled it out and stared. It was a tiny control-wand with what looked like a gold ball bearing magnetically attached to it.

Finn looked at it with mounting excitement. He was sure it was the battery and wand that was used for the discs. 'What's that?' he gasped hoarsely, his throat feeling tight with tension.

'Dunno,' said Richard with a puzzled frown on his face. 'I remember now I found it in my pyjama pocket when I got up this morning. Then I suppose I put it in my trousers when I got dressed.'

A horrible thought crossed Finn's mind. 'Your mum didn't put your pyjamas in the wash, did she?' Whatever would happen to it in a washing machine?

Richard shook his head. 'I don't think so. Anyway, she'd have said something.' He turned it over in his hands. 'What is it anyway?'

Finn tried to sound nonchalant. 'Not sure. Let's have a look at it.' He held out his hand and Richard gave it to him. He closed his fingers over it and found he was sweating with hope! He didn't even look at it, but just sat on the disc with it grasped in his hand. He commanded the disc to move forward. Nothing happened. He shut his eyes in despair.

Richard was looking at him strangely. 'It has to be calibrated to your energy,' he remarked suddenly.

Finn didn't even wonder how the other boy knew that. It must be a memory from Richard's night-time experiences.

Suddenly his friend said, 'It's coming back to me. I'm remembering.' He put his hand on his forehead as if he was seeing things through the dimensions. He seemed to be growing taller as he recalled who he truly was. 'Oh my God! Okay Finn, hold the control-wand between your palms. Say this after me, "Record the following name – Finn White."'

Finn repeated the words.

'Now date of birth.'

Finn said his date of birth.

'Put the wand to each eye in turn and say "left eye", then "right eye". That photographs your iris and registers it.'

Finn did this.

'Now make sure it is charged. You should see a green light.'

Finn turned the tiny square over and nodded.

'Then slot it into the appropriate place on the disc.'

'Ah,' said Finn. 'It isn't a proper disc, so there's nowhere to slot it. Can I just hold it in my hand?'

'Where did the disc come from?' asked Richard suspiciously.

'I made it,' confessed Finn and told him how. The two boys looked at each other as if assessing who they truly were.

'Okay, try holding the wand,' suggested Richard quietly.

Finn sat on the tray and said his name, then told it to fly. In the second they waited for a response it seemed as if every bird was quiet, every animal held its breath. Then the disc vibrated slightly and slowly rose thirty centimetres in the air.

'Yes!' shouted Finn triumphantly.

'Oh!' gasped Richard despite himself. He'd been in some faraway space as he'd given the instructions to connect the computer to the mainframe. Now he could hardly believe what he was seeing. Finn was sitting cross-legged on the disc as it floated gently down the hill. He swerved round a tree and over a bush, then zoomed along by the railway line. Finn wished his friends at school could see him now. Eventually he remembered that Richard was patiently watching and instructed the disc to go back to him.

'Do you think it would take us both if we got on together?' he asked his friend.

Richard nodded eagerly. He was itching to have a go so he squeezed behind Finn, hanging half off the disc. 'Hold onto my waist, Richard,' shouted Finn and then gave the instructions to take off. The plate wobbled under their combined weight but then moved slowly up into the air. It was fun, though somewhat uncomfortable with the two of them on it together.

Because it was a misty day there were very few people about, which was lucky. At first they were wary about being seen but soon they forgot about other people and twisted and turned and even tried to race a train.

Eventually the battery started running low, so they headed for Finn's house while trying to persuade the disc to go higher. They reached the three-metre maximum height and were hovering over the fence at the end of Finn's garden when they heard a loud shout. Finn recognized Blake's voice as his brother yelled, 'What are you doing? Come down at once!' as he raced down the garden towards them. Finn was so startled that he jumped and the disc tipped. Richard tried to hold on but slipped off, narrowly missing the White family's startled cat as he crashed down, landing on his arm. Finn landed on top of him. His brother, who was running too fast, tripped headlong, hitting his head on the path, and sat up groggily with blood pouring everywhere. Finn saw the blood and fainted. The cat howled and ran for his life.

A neighbour who had seen what happened called an ambulance, then scrambled over the fence to help while his wife called their mother's mobile.

Later in hospital Richard had an X-ray, which showed he had broken his collarbone. His arm was put into a sling. Blake was treated for cuts and concussion while Finn sported some bruises and felt an idiot for fainting.

The neighbour was certainly not going to tell anyone that he had seen them flying on a giant frisbee – people would think him mad! Anyway, he decided, he must have imagined what he had seen, especially as the disc had seemingly vanished into thin air. When Blake muttered something about the boys flying above the fence, everyone thought the concussion had temporarily driven him out of his right mind.

As for Finn and Richard, they said they had been climbing a tree and had fallen off into the garden.

For some time the cat kept looking nervously up into the air to see what danger might come crashing from the skies, but he's getting over it now.

CHAPTER 13

VAZ PLAYS A TRICK

Finn felt elated that they had made the flying discs work but terrible about Richard breaking his collarbone. He felt sick every time he thought of it. Last time he had seen his friend he had looked white with pain. He kept wondering if they could bring back some technology from Sirius that would help Richard.

Finn was sure Captain Ambrose would be angry with him for bringing back the technology and, even worse, flying on the discs where people could see them, but even so that night he sat in bed wishing the captain would come.

He tried to send telepathic messages to Agapay and Vaz but it felt as if he was hitting a brick wall. But he was not. He was about to give up and turn his light out when he saw a shimmering light from the corner of his eye. Agapay materialized. 'How did you learn to do that?' he gasped.

She grinned. 'Just practice!' Then her face became concerned. 'Why were you calling me?'

'You heard me?'

'Heard you! You nearly deafened me.'

Finn flushed. Then he told her the whole story.

'You idiot!' she exclaimed but when she saw his face she softened. 'Oh well, boys will be boys,' she said. It was her mother's expression when talking about her younger brothers.

'Do you think we can get some help for Richard from Sirius?' Finn asked. 'They said we'd be visiting the hospital next time we go there.'

'Not if they show us the inter-dimensional specs first,' the girl retorted. 'I really want to see those.' She sighed. 'But you're right. We need help for Richard if we can get it. So let's both try together to call Captain Ambrose.'

So they closed their eyes and focused on the captain, repeating

his name in their minds. Almost immediately he teleported into the room.

'You called me?' His face was calm but his bright blue eyes were twinkling as if he knew everything that had happened. The children both nodded and looked at each other.

At last Finn said, 'It was my fault that Richard broke his collarbone. Can we help him?'

'You mean you want to discover future technology from Sirius to heal his break?' questioned Captain Ambrose, correctly reading his mind.

Finn nodded without much hope but Agapay butted in eagerly. 'Would that be possible?'

And to their surprise the captain said, 'Why not? Follow me!'

As he disappeared they found themselves being pulled through the wall into the spacecraft. Unexpectedly, Captain Ambrose accompanied them into it. He punched MEDICAL DEPARTMENT, SIRIUS into the computer and sat back. The children noticed that he seemed to be finding something very amusing, but when he spoke next he was quite serious.

'You need to know we are working with spiritual technology that can heal anything, whether it is emotional, mental or physical. When the new healing methods come forward no one will be ill or disabled.'

'What about injuries to the spine?' asked Agapay, who knew someone who used a wheelchair as the result of an accident.

'Oh yes. You'll be able to repair spinal damage.' Agapay's eyes were bright as she thought of her mum. 'Please let them find something to help her soon,' she prayed silently.

Finn was unusually quiet. 'It feels strange to be going without Vaz. Not fair somehow.'

'I know,' agreed Agapay. 'I was thinking that too.' A smile flitted across the captain's face.

Suddenly they both felt as if a fly was tickling their noses. At the same moment they twitched and tried to brush it away, but the tickling moved to their cheeks.

'Get off!' said Finn crossly, wafting the invisible fly away.

They heard a chuckle. It was unmistakably Vaz's voice.

'He's here!' yelled Agapay in delight. 'Come on Vaz, make yourself visible.'

And their friend appeared in front of them, his hands still stretched out and his fingers tickling their faces!

'You're not supposed to use your invisibility gift to play tricks,' Agapay remonstrated with mock severity.

Vaz looked at the captain, who shrugged and responded, 'I think fun is a good use of a gift,' and they all laughed.

CHAPTER 14

HOSPITAL ON SIRIUS

Si met them as usual. As they ran over to him a shining blue and yellow craft, like nothing they had seen before, appeared from thin air and purred to a stop in front of them. It was round and huge with a domed top and oval windows.

'The medical centre is on a distant part of the star cluster so we're going by bus!' he explained with a grin.

'A bus!' They looked at one another in astonishment. On the front was a notice that said ZONE 10 – MEDICAL RESEARCH. There were half a dozen beings sitting inside it.

'Some bus!' exclaimed Vaz.

Finn had already stepped into it and was looking in surprise at the comfortable interior with luxurious seats and thick coverings on the floor. Their fellow travellers were mostly Sirians with large heads and ears but there was one thin blue being who smiled jovially and introduced himself as Pacca from the Pleiades.

'There's no driver!' pointed out Agapay.

Everyone laughed in a kindly way and Si explained that everything was controlled remotely. 'I called the bus when you arrived. It only took seconds to come and pick us up.'

Already the bus was moving silently and as fast as light toward the medical centre.

'Why didn't we go directly to the hospital in the spacecraft?' Finn wanted to know.

'Because I thought you'd like to experience a bus ride,' replied Si. 'We are travelling on a wavelength above family-sized transports. The technology for a perfect transport system is available here on Sirius and we are just waiting for the people on Earth to be ready. Then you can have buses like this too.' He paused. 'Ah, here we are. Off we get.'

As the children entered the pyramid that housed the medical

centre they were enfolded in a soft blue light and felt soothed by it.

'We want to know how to help Richard mend his broken collarbone quickly,' Finn reminded Si.

'I know but I want to show you something first.' A door opened and they found themselves in a round chamber. On the wall in front of them was something that looked like a huge mirror.

'That's a diagnostic machine,' explained Si. 'It works on every level and explains the cause of any ill-health within you. Who'd like to try it?'

The boys hesitated but Agapay stepped forward. 'I will.'

'Very well. I want you to stand in front of the machine. Just relax. You will be bombarded by all sorts of coloured light rays – a bit like your X-rays but totally harmless and much more targeted.'

'Okay,' the girl agreed and stood in front of the mirror. Immediately colours flowed into her and from her. A pleasant voice started to commentate. 'Reading for Agapay Stevens. Physical levels – scanning down the body.'

They could see her outline and now grey blobs showed on her head, her eyes and in her stomach. The voice continued, 'Hair healthy but washed with shampoo containing harmful chemicals. Will affect the brain in approximately twenty-two years unless changed. Eyes tense due to reading in poor light. Will need glasses in three years. Digestion good but eating of junk food causing disruption in energy in stomach. Analysis herewith and suggested good diet. Otherwise physically healthy.' There was a whirr and a printout appeared from a slit by the machine.

'Emotional levels,' continued the voice. The picture changed and now a dark energy showed over her middle. 'Some anger from childhood ages 3–5 caused by jealousy of sibling. As a result heavy energy lodged in liver. To cleanse use aquamarine ray with sound healing.

Inherited and genetic levels. Mother's side—'

Agapay stepped back, rather shaken. 'I think I've had enough for now,' she said. 'But it is extraordinary. Does anger really cause illness and can you heal it with technology?'

Si explained that happiness is a light vibration that flows through the body but anger has a slow heavy frequency, which blocks the flow in an organ if it is not released. If it isn't dealt with it eventually causes illness. He led them to a cubicle with a couch in it and asked Agapay to lie down.

'This computer makes the perfect notes to break up heavy frequencies and then bring the organs into harmony. After that the colours will fine-tune you in accordance with your original blueprint of perfect health.'

He programmed something into the computer and placed a tiny micro-enhancer onto her body. As she lay there a deep low sound vibrated through her and a white-aquamarine ray poured into her. She looked as if she had fallen asleep. Then the light switched off and the sound stopped. Agapay opened her eyes and sat up.

Si handed her a glass of pure water. 'Drink this. Then we'll go and look in the mirror again.'

The girl thanked him and drank the water. She looked rather spaced out as she rose from the couch and followed Si back to the mirror. When it was switched on they could all see that the grey blobs had disappeared completely and light was flowing through her. Her eyes were huge as she watched the image.

The boys were strangely quiet. 'Could we bring Richard here?' Finn asked at last.

Si explained that all Richard's energy was being used for the time being to heal his collarbone, so he did not have enough to apport to Sirius. 'And no, he can't come in the spacecraft. That is not for him,' he said gently but firmly.

The boys looked dejected. 'Well, please can we see how you heal broken bones?' asked Finn humbly. 'There must be something we can do for him!'

Agapay felt so great after her healing experience that she almost danced to the room where they knitted bones together. Again Si explained that certain combinations of sounds and colour frequencies stimulate nerves and help tissue grow more quickly. 'Watch this,' he said. 'It's in double time and they are pulsing

H-rays, which are faster frequency light rays than you can access yet on Earth.' They were shown a picture of a woman with a newly broken leg. Specific sounds and pulsing H-rays were being focused on the break and the children saw the crack in the bone come together seamlessly in front of their eyes. The woman got off the couch and walked!

'Isn't that possible for Richard's collarbone?' asked Finn. 'If you could give us the sounds, wouldn't that make a difference?'

'You need the H-light too,' Si told him. 'But you are right. The sounds alone would help.' He paused and thought deeply. 'Look, take this mini portable H-ray pulser. Be careful, don't overdo it. No more than five minutes and bring it back next time.'

He handed Finn a tiny silver capsule. 'It's voice-activated. Tell it five minutes for a broken collarbone and while it is on you make the sounds.' He went through the correct sounds with them until he was sure they would remember them.

Suddenly they were longing to help Richard and for the first time ever they wanted to leave Sirius and go home.

As usual Si read their minds. 'Okay, we won't bother with the bus transport. I'll call your spaceship.' He spoke into the screen that appeared above his watch.

Instantly they saw the spaceship appear in front of them. 'Bye Si,' they called as they leapt aboard and were gone.

VISITING RICHARD

That evening Finn called to see Richard. The boy was very pleased to see him, partly because he was bored and his broken bone hurt but more because he wanted to talk over the extraordinary thing that had happened. Even though he had flown on the disc he still didn't quite believe it.

Once they were in his bedroom with the door shut and were sure Richard's mother wasn't going to knock yet again to see if they wanted anything, Finn focused on Agapay and Vaz, mentally calling them in. He could tell that they were trying to come, but for a few moments they flickered in and out like a television programme that is finding it hard to make a connection.

At last they were fully in the room, Vaz in his old blue sweater and Agapay with a silver net over her hair that matched her silver tights. Richard might be used to seeing people appearing in his dream world but in his ordinary life it still gave him a shock!

Agapay greeted him with, 'Hi Richard, remember me? I'm Agapay. We're here to heal your collarbone,' as if this was the most normal thing in the world.

'And I'm Vaz,' added the boy.

Somewhere in the back of his mind, Richard knew these two both looked familiar. 'H-heal my co-collarbone?' he stammered, taken aback.

'If that's all right with you?' Agapay asked politely.

'Well yes,' muttered the boy. 'That's okay, I suppose.'

The three children put their hands over Richard's shoulder without touching it. Then Finn got out the capsule-shaped H-ray machine and commanded, 'Five minutes for a broken collarbone.' He paused and added, 'Please.' Just in case. Then they all concentrated on making the sounds they had been given. While they were doing this they pictured the bone healed. After five minutes the pulsing on the machine stopped and they fell silent.

'It's finished,' declared Finn. 'How does it feel, Richard?'

The boy focused on his collarbone. Then he moved his arm and shoulder around, gingerly at first, then more confidently. 'I can't feel any pain,' he said in surprise. 'Wow!'

At that moment they heard his mother outside the door and the handle turned. There was no time for Agapay or Vaz to vanish. Quick as a flash they dived behind the bed just as Richard's mum entered. She had untidy sandy hair, freckles and glasses and was a plump version of her son.

'Hello you two,' she beamed at Finn and Richard. 'I've brought you some lemonade and chocolate biscuits.'

Finn thought about the body scanner and what it said about sugar. When on Sirius he had resolved to cut out sugar and junk, but faced with chocolate biscuits he decided that just once would not hurt. 'Thank you,' he responded politely, hoping she would leave the room quickly. But she did not.

She sat on the end of Richard's bed and talked. Finn couldn't think straight. What if she saw Agapay and Vaz? He muttered some answers to her questions.

Vaz loved chocolate biscuits and was itching to reach out and take one. Worse, his leg had gone to sleep as he crouched behind the bed, centimetres from Richard's mother. Agapay dug him in the ribs and mouthed, 'Make us invisible.' Of course! He had forgotten about his gift. In seconds he had made both himself and Agapay invisible.

With relief, Vaz stood up as quietly as he could – but not silently enough. Richard's mother looked sharply in the direction of the sound but of course there was nothing to be seen. Vaz couldn't stop himself, though. He leaned over and picked up a chocolate biscuit – to Richard's mother's eyes, it seemed to fly up off the plate all by itself and vanish in mid-air.

Agapay smothered a giggle from behind the bed. Finn looked as innocent as he could and Richard just stared straight ahead.

Richard's mother put her hand to her head. She looked as though she thought she was going mad. Then she got up and stumbled to the door, leaving them in peace.

Later that evening she commented to her husband that Finn was decidedly weird, even though he looked cute with all that lovely blond hair. It was a good job Finn did not hear that! And she could not get over how much better Richard looked. He had taken his sling off because he said his collarbone did not hurt any more, and was acting as if it was completely better. 'After one day!' she said. 'It's impossible!'

CHAPTER 15

BATTLE OF THE DRAGONS

A few days later Finn was supposed to be doing his homework in the dining room but really he was thinking about the inter-dimensional audio specs and Richard's collarbone. His brother, Blake, was upstairs having a shower, so luckily Finn was on his own when there came a loud banging on the window. He looked up sharply and could hardly believe his eyes.

Tapping on the glass with its beak was Finn's fire dragon, Flame. The three children had earned their fire dragons after the success of their quest to bring back the Golden Trumpet some time ago, but they did not see them very often.

The boy's face lit up as he dashed to the window and threw it open. 'Flame! I haven't seen you for ages. What are you doing here?' he cried. Then he saw Agapay and Vaz perched on their dragons, hovering above the fence at the end of the garden waiting for him. His stomach somersaulted and he knew there was trouble even before Captain Ambrose appeared outside the window.

The captain spoke urgently. 'There's an attack on Sirius by a flock of Deceptri. Hurry up. We need you. Get on your dragon and I'll explain as we go.'

Finn's knees trembled as he clambered out of the window and scrambled onto Flame. He hoped his mother didn't come in to check on his homework – but he was even more terrified of what lay ahead. Sirius under attack!

He tried to act as if he was calm. He patted his dragon's head and murmured, 'You've grown, Flame.'

'Yes, I grow as you gain in strength and confidence,' his dragon replied. Finn was surprised and pleased but he didn't have time to respond before Captain Ambrose on his huge purple beast drew up beside him. The great winged creatures surged forward in hot pursuit of Vaz and Agapay, who were streaking ahead.

The captain shouted, 'The Deceptri look like huge black crows with serpent bodies. They have enormous red eyes and they contain all the fear and hatred of the universe gathered together. They want to knock Sirius out and take all of its knowledge. That will prevent the growth of Earth and many other stars and planets. We have to stop it. You and Vaz and Agapay must stay together and watch out for each other.'

'But why us? What can we do?'

'You can direct the dragons to burn up the fear the Deceptri send out. But more importantly than that, human hearts can love and it is only love that can change the universe.'

Finn asked impatiently, 'Why don't we go straight to Sirius? We're wasting time.'

'No! The fire dragons are under the command of Thor and his Thunder Gods. And the great Archangel Gabriel is in charge of all Fire. He will talk to us all first.'

Finn nodded that he understood, even though he did not agree, and urged Flame to fly faster.

Ahead he could see hundreds of thousands of flames where fire dragons massed in a vast desert surrounded by mountains.

Captain Ambrose shouted, 'Good luck!' and wheeled his purple dragon away to take his place beside a Thunder God at the head of his squadron. The captain looked tiny in comparison. Thor sat astride the hugest dragon. It had a scarlet head with an orange body and was the size of a large truck. Each of the squadrons was headed by a Thunder God on an equally enormous dragon.

Finn slotted into a space next to Vaz and Agapay. They could hear the rasping pants and smoker's coughs of the dragons and an occasional roar of fire as one became overexcited.

Finn looked round. A girl with dark untidy curls and a determined little face perched on the dragon beside him. A tiny grey kitten sat on her lap, its ears cocked as if it was listening hard. Finn said, 'Hi' and told her his name.

'I'm Tara,' the girl responded, 'and this is my kitten Ash-ting. He can talk to me. He's magic.' Ash-ting nodded rather majestically

and meowed. Tara confided that she had been on local trips with her dragon but never anything like this. She sounded nervous and Finn told her stoutly to stick with him and his friends and they'd look after her. Tara looked relieved and Agapay and Vaz smiled and gave her a thumbs-up. Ash-ting the kitten stared at them with his big round green eyes as if assessing them. Then he nodded his approval and said something to Tara. She said, 'He says you have the right heart for this battle.'

Finn frowned. There it was again, something about heart.

Vaz looked round. 'Do you think Richard is here?'

'No,' Agapay responded. 'The captain said he's got an air dragon and they are not taking part this time.'

Before they had time to ask questions a trumpet sounded. Everyone sat to attention. The dragons became still and silent. The Thunder Gods grew even taller. And then a bright white light appeared before them. It was so brilliant it lit up the entire desert and yet it did not blind them or hurt their eyes.

'Gabriel,' the whisper flew on the breeze.

The archangel's strong voice addressed them. He spoke of strength, courage and duty. He inspired them with hope, togetherness and a glorious future when the Deceptri were overcome. 'Evil is only deep fear, so keep love and purpose in your hearts for we cannot conquer with fear or force. Fighting for control was the old way in the universe and it does not work.' He paused and his gaze swept across the gathered beings. 'We can only dissolve fear with love. So this will be a war of light and love, for we play by noble rules. I am delighted to announce we have humans among us who can pour love from their hearts.' There was a murmur of surprise and the children felt their hearts glow with warmth, as did the other humans in the army.

Gabriel continued. 'Every one of you will carry one of the new extra-Z phlasic torches that are tuned to the super-spectrum of love. It will fire violet, pink and white P-rays that devour the vibrations of fear. It can soften the bitterest evil if you shoot it directly into the eye of a Deceptri so that it enters their heart.'

Instantly each of the dragon riders found themselves holding a long thin extra-Z phlasic torch, which they were warned to handle with care. The children glanced at each other in surprise and held them cautiously.

Overcoming the Deceptri

The great white light, followed by a million smaller lights, which were Gabriel's angels, rose up and led the way to Sirius. And the dragons ascended as one, huffing orange flames with a roar like a vast train that reverberated through the universe. Nervous people on Earth looked at the dark sky, expecting a tornado or hurricane to engulf them.

The huge flock of black creatures making up the Deceptri was hovering above Sirius. Some of them swept down to attack the pyramids. The Sirians within the pyramids were sending out light to illuminate them, but even over the noise of the battle the children could hear the crash of destruction.

The first wave of dragons poured towards the Deceptri, their flames burning up the dark cloud of fear surrounding them. The dragon riders were aiming violet, pink and white P-rays towards the flying slithering monsters and lights were shooting like fireworks across the sky. Occasionally the aim was true and love entered a red eye and penetrated the heart of the creature, which would shriek and howl as it started to see the light for the first time. Other Deceptri tried to bite the dragons and their riders.

As the battle became more intense some dragons fell as they were surrounded and cut off by the Deceptri.

Archangel Gabriel was clear and strong. As the second wave of dragons raced towards the cloud of dark creatures he sounded a melodious note of hope and encouragement. The children stayed together, clinging to their winged steeds, whooping, shouting directions and firing their extra-Z phlasic torches carefully.

Suddenly Finn saw a space ahead and in the blackness he saw one of the Deceptri's huge red eyes. He directed his dragon towards it and tried to radiate love from his heart as they plunged into the darkness that stank of fear. As Finn launched at it, the creature closed its eyelid so he could not see the eye but he felt the ball of jelly and clawed into it, trying to manoeuvre his Z torch into position to fire. The creature struggled to bite him but ignoring its screams the boy jabbed his fingers tighter into the slippery form. The eye opened again and glowered at him with venom.

Suddenly Tara saw what was happening. She shook back her curly hair and forced her dragon forward. As fast as a hawk she jabbed her Z torch into the Deceptri's eye and tried to fire. The creature was wriggling so hard that she couldn't pull the trigger. But Ash-ting, her kitten, leapt onto the Deceptri and bit it without compunction. It oozed slimy black goo and collapsed like a punctured balloon, moaning pathetically.

'You're just afraid,' muttered Finn to the creature with sudden compassion, and he and Tara simultaneously shot a P-ray of love into its heart.

To their immense astonishment a pure white bird with a golden breast emerged from the heart of the black body and spread out its wings. It soared into the air until they could not see it any longer.

Tara and Finn stared at each other in amazement and hope.

At that moment they saw and heard the third wave of dragons sweeping towards the Deceptri. The noise and fire was terrible, like a thousand trains crashing. Below them they were aware of a blazing inferno.

Then quite suddenly the Deceptri collapsed, defeated.

The dragons and their riders withdrew into their ranks to watch the end. Occasionally a black creature would escape from the fire and the humans opened their hearts and sent them love.

Each time a white-winged dovelike creature emerged everyone cheered with joy.

The four children on their dragons were asked to step forward and they received a round of dragon applause, which sounded like cough, cough, cough. One hour later choirs of angels sang over Sirius and the air became calm and clear.

The battle was won.

FINN'S FLU

Finn felt very weary as they flapped slowly back to Earth on their dragons. First he called goodbye to the feisty Tara and her little grey kitten, who waved a paw to him before they glided down towards their home. Then Vaz on his dragon zoomed off in his own direction. Finally Agapay waved goodbye.

He was pleased to see his house below and Flame swooped gently down to deposit him in his garden. The boy slid off and gave his dragon a big hug, then waved as it soared up into the sky again. 'Call me any time, Finn,' called Flame.

'I will,' shouted back the boy, watching his friend disappear from sight.

He yawned as he walked up the path thinking about finishing his homework. Unfortunately, when he climbed through the dining room window his mother was standing by the table with her hands on her hips waiting for him. She had been watching him in the garden.

'Try telling me you were practising to be an actor, hugging an invisible person and waving goodbye to them?' she said sarcastically. 'All I can say is, you'd better get good marks for your homework.'

Finn said nothing and looked at his shoes. This was not the time to ask if he could have a little grey kitten.

But he never did give in his homework because he woke up next morning feeling terrible. 'I think I've got flu,' he groaned to his mother and she took one look at him and believed him. 'You've got a temperature. You'll be in bed for a couple of days.'

When he was nearly better Captain Ambrose came to see Finn in the night. 'How are you feeling?' the man asked him solicitously. 'You did a really good job. We are proud of you.'

'Thanks,' Finn smiled, 'but why was I so ill?'

'Your body was clearing out the negativity you absorbed from the Deceptri. Agapay and Vaz have had "flu" too.'

'I see.' Finn understood just why he had been so unwell.

'Even the dragons had to clear out the horrible energy. They've been croaking and coughing all week and feeling very sorry for themselves.'

'Poor old Flame,' Finn thought and laughed despite himself. 'What about Tara and Ash-ting?'

'She was not so badly affected because her kitten protected her.'

Finn was astonished and the captain explained. 'Oh yes, cats protect their families from dark energy.'

'Do they!' the boy exclaimed, then added after a pause, 'Anyway, we did it. We saved Sirius.'

'Yes you did. There was quite a bit of damage,' Captain Ambrose admitted, 'but it will all be clear by the time you are ready to go again. And the doves are now working with us. Next time—'

'We'll see the IDAS?' finished Finn with a grin of triumph.

'Yes!' agreed the captain. 'At last you can try the inter-dimensional audio specs.'

'I feel better already,' said Finn, and laughed.

CHAPTER 16

INTER-DIMENSIONAL AUDIO SPECS (IDAS)

It was two weeks before they returned to Sirius. 'Let's programme the spacecraft to hover over it before we land, so we can see what damage there is,' suggested Agapay and the boys agreed this was a good idea. They peered out of the windows as their craft circled slowly and to their relief, they saw that most of the mess had been repaired.

As always they were overjoyed to see Si and Richard waiting for them, this time in a yellow transport colourfully decorated with animals and birds. They wondered if Richard knew anything about the battle against the Deceptri, but before they had a chance to speak the boy started to tell them about the IDAS. 'You just ask for the dimension you want to tune in to or the being you wish to access and you will actually be able to see and talk to them. Isn't that amazing! It's a bit like television. You select your programme and you're automatically on that wavelength, but with the IDAS you are in that dimension.'

Si laughed. 'Hey, don't you think these guys might like to get to the lab first?'

But they all assured him they wanted to see the audio specs now.

Richard flushed with pleasure. 'I thought so. I brought three pairs with me. Here you are.'

He handed them a pair each and explained that you just put them on and tuned the computer within them with your voice.

'I want to see fairies,' announced Agapay into the screen quickly before anyone else had time to speak.

Immediately the children found themselves in a glade alive with trees, ferns and flowers, a little stream and soft green grass. Beautiful lights about thirty centimetres tall flittered among the flowers and they could see that in each one was a little winged fairy.

'Oh wow!' gasped Agapay, reaching out a hand. A bright red fairy left the poppy she had been tending and landed on Agapay's palm. 'Hello,' she said in a high clear voice, 'My name is Poppy. Welcome to our world.'

'Er, thank you for letting us come,' responded Agapay, for the boys seemed to have lost their voices and were staring at the fairy.

Finn recovered his wits first. 'What do you do?'

'We tend the flowers and play with children and have lots of fun.' Suddenly they found themselves surrounded by fairies dancing and laughing, and immediately they too felt happy and joyful. 'We also help the unicorns sometimes,' added Poppy.

The children looked at each other. 'Unicorns?'

'Yes, unicorns are real but they are very noble and pure. They work with people who want to help others. We fairies cooperate with angels too and all the other elementals.'

'What about dragons?' asked Vaz. 'We've got our own dragons.'

'Yes, dragons. They are wonderful too and absolutely enormous sometimes. Oh look! You called them with your energy. Here they come.'

Into their world flew Flame, Pitta and Bizz. The children screamed with delight as their dragons landed beside them, grinning. Yes, it is possible for a dragon to grin! The fairies tickled them and played with them until even the serious dragons were chuckling and trying not to breathe out fire, which might have set light to the trees.

'How about ogres?' said Finn quickly. Immediately they found themselves in a huge forest where the trees were dark and close together. They felt very small and a bit scared.

'Ee!' squeaked Agapay when a sticky vine wound itself round her leg.

'Sh!' whispered the boys, who were trying to appear brave.

Around them they could hear crashing and booming and they weren't sure if it was trees falling, ogres moving about or loud voices talking. They crept towards a space where the trees were wider apart and saw that the forest opened into a clearing. In the middle sat two giants, each with one huge eye in the centre of its forehead. They must have been seven metres tall and they were arguing.

As they shouted the breath coming from their mouths was like a gale-force wind. No wonder the trees were swaying and branches were cracking and banging!

Suddenly one stopped and sniffed. ''Umans?' The other one sniffed too. 'Right you are, 'umans. Pre-dinner snacks!' He leapt up and the ground shook as if there was an earthquake coming.

The children's knees felt like water.

'Fairies!' screamed Agapay.

'Angels!' shouted Finn.

'Home!' yelled Vaz.

Instantly, white-faced and trembling, they were standing by the yellow transport surrounded by fairies and three angels. They sighed with relief and amazement when they saw them.

The angels had huge soft wings and golden light shone around them. 'Wow, you're just like the pictures of angels,' commented Finn.

Everyone laughed and somehow they relaxed and colour flowed back into their faces.

'I am your guardian angel,' one of the angels said to Finn. 'Please be careful what you ask for. I try to help you all the time but ogres are a bit of a challenge.'

Finn felt embarrassed but only for a moment, for such love flowed from the angel that he knew he was not in trouble. He smiled.

'Do we all have a guardian angel?' asked Agapay.

'Indeed you do. Everyone does. And here I am,' her angel responded, gently putting a wing round the girl. 'And we love you whatever you do.' Agapay snuggled into her and felt very safe.

'There's nothing you can do that can stop us from loving you,' agreed the third angel. 'We are constantly whispering to you what is the best thing to do.'

'And we arrange for you to meet the right people at the right time.'

'Just ask us for help and we'll do it – if it is right for you.'

Finn felt the most wonderful warm glow of being safe and happy. He could see from Agapay and Vaz's faces that they felt the same.

The bright red poppy fairy flew quickly round them, catching their attention. 'Si wants you back now,' she told them.

'Remember to ask us for help, even if you can't see us. We're always with you,' the three angels reminded them and vanished. Poppy and all the fairies simply were not there any more.

Si and Richard were sitting in the yellow transport. 'What do you think of the IDAS?' asked Richard.

But for a few minutes the children could not even speak.

At last Finn thought of the angels. 'Amazing! But is all that stuff real?'

At that moment a little white feather fell out of the sky and landed on his hand. 'A feather,' screeched Agapay. 'An angel feather. It has actually landed on you.'

'I think that answers your question,' said Si. 'Oh yes, there are beings living on all the wavelengths and dimensions. The worlds interpenetrate each other but because you are at a different frequency you aren't even aware of them.'

'Make sure you tune in to the wavelengths that are okay,' advised Richard. 'You don't want to be around nasties. I had a horrible time when I thought I was being clever and called in a monster. Now I mainly stick with elementals, angels and unicorns.'

'And Masters,' suggested Agapay.

'Yes.'

'And spirits of loved ones?'

'Well, carefully,' Si replied.

'And aliens?'

'The helpful ones only,' Si said firmly. 'Perhaps you need a little tuition before you use those IDAS again!'

CHAPTER 17

FINN'S BROTHER: AN ACCIDENT

Finn was woken by a terrible commotion in his house. His mother was crying. The phone was ringing. There were strange voices coming from downstairs. He knew straight away that something awful had happened.

He got out of bed and went to investigate. That was when he learned that his brother Blake had been involved in a terrible car crash and had been rushed to hospital by ambulance.

His parents were about to race to the hospital and Finn had to go with them as there was no one else at home to look after him.

Several ghastly hours later, after waiting impatiently in the hospital's white corridors for news, they learned that Blake had broken his back and might never walk again. Finn felt cold and numb. He could not believe that his brother's life could change for ever like that in one instant. He kept thinking about the spiritual technology of the future. Couldn't something be done?

His parents made him go to school next day but he sat miserably looking at his desk and didn't want to play football or speak to anyone.

When he got home his parents were at the hospital and his grandmother had come to look after him. She had changed overnight from a cheerful person to a grey-faced old lady. It was sad. Her dog, Toffee, was an elderly but clever mongrel and usually Finn played with her a lot but today he didn't have the heart to do so.

He told his grandmother he was going to do his homework in his bedroom. Then he sat on the bed with his head in his hands, mentally calling over and over again to Captain Ambrose.

At last a light flickered in the corner of the room and the captain materialized. He clearly knew what had happened to Blake, for his eyes were full of concern.

'We can't bring the future back to now,' he explained but Finn would not accept it. 'You said that time goes faster when you are happy,' he argued.

'That's true. Then you change dimension and time speeds up,' conceded the spaceman.

'And if you move to a much higher frequency everything happens at the same time,' pursued Finn. 'I heard you say that!'

The captain nodded. 'That is right. But you have to be *able* to move into a higher dimension.'

'Well, we did with the inter-dimensional audio specs.' Finn was not going to give up.

Captain Ambrose thought deeply. It was as if Finn's dogged determination to help Blake had affected him. 'Miracles happen all the time,' he muttered to himself. 'They happen when higher vibrations consume lower ones.' He looked Finn in the eye. 'Okay. Your love for your brother has drawn in new possibilities. Let's go to Sirius.'

Finn felt himself being pulled through the wall into the spacecraft as the captain faded out of sight.

He was alone in the spacecraft for a few moments until Vaz and Agapay arrived. Finn had already programmed the flight computer to go to THE MEDICAL DEPARTMENT, SIRIUS and as soon as his friends appeared he shouted, 'Go!'

The journey only took seconds because they went through the nearest wormhole. No one asked about Blake but he saw from their faces that they already knew. Agapay gave him a hug, while Vaz sort of clapped him awkwardly on the shoulder. When they arrived at their destination Si and Richard were waiting for them with double flying discs.

Si enveloped Finn in a great reassuring bear grip. Then Richard motioned Finn to get up behind him on his disc while Agapay and Vaz jumped onto the spare double disc and Si flew off in front of them, leading the way.

Captain Ambrose was waiting for them in the department where they had learned about mending bones. This time he took them into a side section where the computer programme radiated intensely coloured laser lights, sounds and electric impulses to repair severed nerves.

'First I want to show you the possibilities,' he said. 'This man broke his back in a fall and you will be able to see how it was healed.' There was a huge screen in front of them and as the captain activated it a picture of a man appeared. He was lying on a couch and they could see inside his body.

They watched in awe as the computer searched for his perfect health blueprint, which showed up on the screen superimposed over the image of the man.

Then the computer radiated lights, sounds and impulses, and they observed as the nerves gently drew together and reattached, the bones knitted and the muscles relaxed. Eventually the man stood up. Everyone cheered.

Finn's stomach was churning. He kept thinking, 'That could be Blake.' He turned in time to see Si and Captain Ambrose look at each other. A flash of light passed between them.

Captain Ambrose picked up a watch and strapped it to Finn's wrist. 'You must set it to Blake's perfect health blueprint,' he murmured. The boy knew that the 'watch' was a computer that held the spiritual technology to heal Blake. 'Thank you,' he whispered, at the same time terrified and delighted.

The children talked excitedly all the way back to the spacecraft, but they did not foresee the next challenge. Blake was to have an emergency operation that evening and only his parents were allowed to be in the hospital. Finn could not get to his brother with the computer so they could not do the healing. What could they do? Finn felt all the hope draining away from him.

Later that evening Richard called at Finn's house. His grandmother opened the door and sent the boy up to his room. 'Please, don't disturb us, Granny. We've got to catch up on homework,' Finn called downstairs, shutting the door firmly.

The two boys focused on Agapay and Vaz, calling them urgently, and they arrived at exactly the same moment.

'They won't let me see Blake,' explained Finn sadly, 'so I can't even try the computer on him. It needs to be done immediately or the nerves will die.'

Richard put his hand in his pocket and drew something out. 'I managed to bring these with me from Sirius,' he said, opening his hand and displaying two tiny gold balls. 'These are the new batteries I've been working on. They'll power a double disc and I can operate it from my watch.'

No one responded until Vaz said, 'Great. But what use is that?'

'Don't you see?' said Agapay excitedly, suddenly getting it. 'Finn can materialize two double discs and we can go to the hospital. And Vaz can make us invisible, so we can get into the operating theatre to use the programme on Blake!'

Suddenly everyone was talking at once. Then Finn said, 'But we can't all go.'

'We all need to be there,' contradicted Richard. 'We have to add our energy to focus with the healing programme.'

'Yes!' the others shouted so enthusiastically that Toffee barked and Finn's grandmother called upstairs. 'Is everything all right?' And after that they were quiet as mice; a bit too quiet as it turned out.

Saving Blake

Finn started to focus on manifesting the double-sized discs, with the protective rails that Agapay insisted on. As he concentrated the discs appeared in the room. Richard slotted the computer batteries into them and calibrated them to the children's energies via his watch-link.

When they were sure everything was working they got onto the discs, Richard with Finn and Vaz with Agapay. Vaz was just about to make them invisible when they heard footsteps on the stairs. Finn's grandmother was coming up.

They froze. As quickly as he could Vaz made himself, Agapay and their disc invisible – just in time. The knock came and the door opened. 'I thought you were a bit quiet,' Finn's granny said. 'I've brought you some juice and biscuits to keep you going until supper.'

'Thanks Granny,' said Finn, taking the tray quickly.

'What's that?' she asked, eyeing the double disc with protective rails. Richard responded promptly, pushing his glasses up his nose in his most nerdy gesture. 'It's a school project. This is a supersize XPY-calibrated turbo motivator. We are calculating the gravity per 6HZ at 2% resistance for our science homework.' He saw Finn's grandmother's eyes glaze over and persisted. 'Would you like me to explain in more detail?'

'Don't overdo it, Richard,' thought Finn, trying to suppress a smile.

But she said, 'Oh you children, you're so clever these days! Come on Toffee. These boys have important work to do.'

'If only you knew,' Finn thought.

But Toffee didn't want to go. She was sniffing round the invisible Agapay and Vaz, whining.

'Silly old girl,' said Finn's grandmother. 'There's no one there.'

'Yes, silly Toffee,' echoed Finn. 'Off you go then.'

At last, very reluctantly and with a final bark at the invisible children, Toffee left the room and the door closed behind her. But a few minutes later, the dog had escaped from the kitchen and was scratching at Finn's bedroom door. She was going to ruin everything.

'Go on Agapay. Use your gift. Talk to the dog,' Finn said. Vaz made the girl visible again and quickly they let the dog in. Agapay explained to Toffee that they were on a special mission and she had an important part to play. She was to keep Finn's grandmother out of the way. Toffee was proud and pleased but she responded that Finn's grandmother was so worried about Blake that she was hardly listening to her.

Agapay had a flash of brilliance. 'Sit on her knee and she'll stroke you and fall asleep because she's so tired,' she suggested.

'I'm not a lapdog,' responded Toffee huffily.

'No, of course not. We can see you are a special, highly intelligent and independent wolf,' replied Agapay. Toffee was so pleased that she was putty in the girl's hands after that. She agreed, Agapay told the others when she recounted the whole conversation, to keep Finn's grandmother out of the way for at least two hours. And with her tail wagging she ran lightly downstairs to start her work.

In seconds the four children were on the double discs again and hovering in the air. But to their dismay they were too big to fly out of the bedroom window. After a frantic whispered debate they realized there was only one thing to do. Vaz made them all invisible yet again and they crept carefully past the kitchen, where Toffee distracted Finn's grandmother by whining for food.

Once outside they soared towards the hospital. They flew over the car park where people were jostling and circling for space. 'Thank goodness for the discs,' muttered Finn and the others agreed. 'Let's get right up to the operating theatre to do the healing programme. Blake will be going in now.'

'Why are we doing it now? Why not after the op?' asked Vaz.

'Because we have to do it as soon as possible to save the nerves and also because he'll be relaxed under anaesthetic so he'll accept the treatment more easily.' Agapay was almost cold in her explanation and it shut Vaz up. He whispered, 'Operating theatre,' to the disc and they flew down the long white corridors.

They accidentally flew through one person, who looked startled as he knew he had felt something but had no idea what had happened!

The doors to the operating theatre were closed. Finn looked at his watch. 'He should be here in two minutes. Let's go in and wait.'

'Wait till the doors are opened. It takes less energy than going through closed doors or walls,' urged Richard. 'We need the energy for Blake.' Finn agreed, though he was feeling very jumpy and rather sick. Oh how he hoped this would work! His friends could obviously not see him, but they could sense his tension.

Then they heard the rumble of the trolley coming down the corridor, surrounded by nurses, and the next second they could

make out Blake's unconscious form lying on it. Finn felt as if he was going to faint. Blake looked dead to him.

'Hold on,' whispered Richard and as the doors opened they manoeuvred the discs carefully through them.

While the surgeons prepared for the operation, the four children hovered above Blake. They decided to start the programme immediately. Richard checked that the computer was set to Blake's perfect health blueprint. He whispered 'Go!' and immediately they could see and sense the pulses emanating from the watch-link towards Finn's brother. A forcefield was gathering round him and they all felt the power of it.

When the surgery started all the children felt faint and queasy, and concentrated very hard on helping Blake in order to stop themselves from being sick. Agapay held grimly to her disc's rails and was glad she had suggested them. Her chest felt tight with hope. If Blake could walk again, then they could surely help her mum. She sighed, then forced herself to concentrate on what was happening on the operating table. The surgeon commented that the nerves did not appear to be as badly damaged as he'd expected. 'I can't understand it,' he said. 'The X-ray shows they were completely severed but they aren't.'

He frowned as he examined the X-ray again. 'And the bruising isn't nearly as bad as you'd expect from an injury like this.'

The children clung to each other in delight. That meant the nerves were already joining and healing.

As the operation progressed the surgeon was becoming increasingly optimistic, and so were the children. They did not turn the watch-link off until the operation was completely finished and then, as the doctors and nurses scrubbed up, they floated round the operating theatre, high-fiving one another.

'We'd better get back,' whispered Finn. 'I don't know how much longer Toffee can keep Granny out of the way.'

On the way out, as they flew down the corridor they passed a waiting room and Finn saw his parents in there. He almost shouted, 'Hi Mum and Dad!' but stopped himself. However, the shock of seeing them there made him visible for a moment and his mother looked up and saw him suspended in the air. 'Finn!' she exclaimed sharply and dug her husband in the ribs. But by the time he had glanced up, Finn had disappeared again.

'You're imagining things, dear. It's all the stress,' said her husband soothingly. But she said, worriedly, 'I wonder if everything's all right. I think I'll just go out and phone Granny to check.' She got up to leave the waiting room and Finn urged the others to race home. 'Fast! Fast as you can go! Before Granny finds me gone!'

CHAPTER 18

Tele-link Communication

Finn was covered in mud, red in the face and very pleased with himself for scoring two goals in the Saturday-morning football match. He was running off the field, high-fiving his teammates, when he saw a boy hunched up in an anorak, sitting on a bench waiting. It was Richard!

Finn felt irritated for a moment. Whatever did he want?

'Just a sec,' he called to his mates and raced across the field to the bench.

'What are you doing here?' he called, more abruptly than he really meant to, and saw Richard hunch further and become even smaller.

'N-nothing,' he stammered and Finn realized how he'd sounded. He remembered how sensitive the boy was and how much he had been teased in the past. He stopped and took a breath. 'Sorry. What did you want?' he asked in a more kindly tone.

Richard eyed him through his fogged-up glasses, lenses as if checking it was all right to speak. At last he muttered, 'Tonight's our last chance before the holidays and I wanted to show you the new tele-link. It's the way we'll all be phoning each other in the future.'

Finn saw how excited Richard was underneath his diffident air. It lit a spark inside him. He sat beside him on the bench. 'Tell me about it?' he said.

And so that afternoon Finn sat in his bedroom waiting for a call from Captain Ambrose. Richard was right. The Christmas holidays were about to start and they would not have a chance to visit Sirius for a while with so much going on.

At last the captain appeared with a smile. 'So your holidays start soon. And Blake will be home from hospital, I hear?'

Finn nodded and responded with a grateful smile. Half the people said Blake's amazing recovery was a miracle; the other half that the original diagnosis had been wrong. Finn knew the truth and he was just glad to have his brother back and learning to walk again. He was on crutches but that was also because of other bones he had broken in the accident. Blake was determined to make a full recovery and when he decided something he put his all into it. There was still a way to go but a black cloud had been lifted from the family.

'I gather Richard wants to show you the new tele-link he and others have been working on?' the captain said.

'Yes, he says we'll all be using it before too long.'

'That's true. And soon more people will become telepathic and then they won't even need a tele-link system. Come on, let's go.'

Seconds later they found themselves in the spacecraft and a few minutes after that Finn, Agapay and Vaz were sitting in a green transport that arrived remotely when Si called it on his watch-link. They were on their way to the tech lab.

The first thing they saw when they arrived in the pyramid were star-shaped objects moving silently across the floors. They changed shape to flow into corners and over furniture. 'They are remote cleaners,' Si told them. 'Every house will have one in due course for dusting and vacuuming carpets. They're powered by solar batteries. Some are remote-controlled but the latest ones clean a room automatically. And that,' he pointed to a blue oblong-shaped thing, 'is an atomic destructor. It dematerializes all rubbish back to its original atomic components so that it vanishes. So there will be no garbage problems in the future – though that one is quite a long way off.'

He picked up a can and a cloth and pushed them into the hole at the top of the atomic destructor. There was a brief whirr and then silence. He opened the lid and they peered in. The machine was empty. The can and cloth had liquidized.

The children looked at each other wonderingly.

'The tele-link,' Si reminded them with a small smile. 'Let's contact Richard in the lab. He's waiting for us.' He pressed his watch-link, put a finger on his forehead, then asked them to do the same thing. Instantly they could see Richard at his desk examining a weird-looking contraption.

Richard saw them connect with him, touched his throat with his finger and said, 'Hi guys, nice to see you. What did you think of the garbage gobbler? Neat, isn't it?'

They all nodded in response and, when he commented on Agapay's new hairstyle, they realized excitedly he could see them as well as hear them. They laughed because you couldn't miss her hair. It was completely outlandish, divided into four bunches, each one striped in different colours. One was green and white, another blue and pink, the third purple and yellow, while the fourth was red and navy – and each bunch was standing out from her head in spikes. For someone so intelligent and cool, she really did have bizarre tastes, Finn thought. To make it worse her T-shirt and jeans were colour-coordinated to her hair – or discorded, according to your perception.

The girl blushed, then laughed with them. 'I was just trying something new,' she responded. 'What do you think of the perfume to go with it?'

Richard sniffed and tried to disguise a cough. That's when they realized the tele-link enabled him to smell them too. Agapay sighed. 'I thought so, it's too sweet. I'll have to try again.'

'You'd be interested in our fashion department,' suggested Richard. 'That's where they are working with technology to produce new materials for the future, both to wear and for other purposes. Look at this.' He said something to his watch-com and they were connected in to a vast, cheerfully coloured factory.

'Wow!' exclaimed Agapay and her eyes lit up. A young woman appeared in the tele-link and introduced herself as Peace. She held up an all-in-one bright blue catsuit. 'This would fit you perfectly, Agapay,' she said and seemed to pass it through thin air to them. All Finn knew was that suddenly Agapay was wearing it and indeed it fitted her like a glove.

'It's perfect,' she breathed. 'I don't feel as if I'm wearing anything but it's light and cool and gorgeous.' She stretched and moved about and the material moved with her.

Peace told her that it was made of material of the future. 'It breathes and stretches and is self- cleaning. The colour won't fade and it keeps you warm or cool, depending on your needs. Also, you can change the colour to anything you want by putting it through a spectrum fixer. This will be very popular in lots of places.'

'What about something more feminine?' Agapay wanted to know.

Peace laughed and held up several breathtaking pieces of clothing that were unlike anything Agapay had ever seen. 'The world is changing,' Peace reminded her. 'Everyone will be able to express themselves in any way they want. While lots will go for the practicality of the outfit you are wearing now, you can be as feminine as you like.'

'I'd love to work with you,' Agapay declared as she found herself wearing her original clothing again. Peace said she was welcome to join them any time.

Agapay was alight with delight. The tight dread she'd had in her chest since her mum became ill melted away completely. Life was full of hope and new possibilities.

While they were talking to Peace, Richard had left his desk and arrived on a disc to greet them. 'What do you think of the tele-link?' he demanded, grinning.

'Amazing,' was the general response and then everyone clamoured to know how it worked. 'Oh, we are starting to work at a super-light level to enable people to tune in to their own innate gifts.'

He turned to Vaz. 'Who would you like to talk to?'

Vaz thought for a moment. 'My dad. He's working away at the moment.'

'Okay, think about him and touch my watch-link,' Richard told him. 'Then touch your throat and your forehead.' Vaz did so and a light shone from his finger into his throat and forehead. Then they heard a mobile ringing. He said. 'Dad! It's Vaz. Where are you?' He saw his father sitting in a row of seats and added, 'Are you on a plane?'

A deep voice replied, 'Yes, I'm on my way home but –' he sounded perplexed – 'My mobile's switched off. You can't take calls on a plane.'

Vaz was getting carried away by what he could see. 'Are you eating a bar of chocolate, Dad? You promised you were on a diet.'

His dad sounded guilty. 'Oh no, no, no,' he lied. Vaz could see him hiding the bar of chocolate under his laptop.

They were all laughing, even Richard, as he touched his watch-com and cut the link.

'Your poor dad,' spluttered Finn. 'He's going to wonder what on earth was happening.' And they all collapsed with laughter again.

'It just shows how careful you have to be,' warned Si. 'There will be no secrets and nowhere to hide when the new spiritual technology is invented on Earth. Little things and big things will be revealed.'

'Some people can receive the tele-link already without a phone if they are psychic,' said Richard. 'Can you think of anyone?'

Finn had a sudden flash. 'How about Tara? You know, the girl with the little grey kitten who was on the dragon next to us when we fought the Deceptri. But I don't know her number.'

The others fell about laughing once more.

'You don't need a number with a tele-link. You just think about them,' explained Si and Finn could have kicked himself but he laughed with the others all the same. 'It's a different way of thinking,' he complained.

'Of course it is,' agreed Si. 'It will come gradually to Earth but here it's being thrust on you and you haven't had time to get used to it.'

Finn felt better.

'Now think about Tara and touch the watch-link, then your throat. It will give you a blue electro-light impulse that will activate your natural telepathic gift. Then put your finger on your forehead and activate your clairvoyant abilities.' Finn did so and a clear picture appeared, of Tara sitting with Ash-ting the kitten under an oak tree. She was talking to a little being who he assumed was an elf!

'Hello,' he said excitedly. 'Hello Tara.'

The girl looked round as if looking for something, then shook back her dark curls. 'She has felt the buzz in her forehead telling her that someone is communicating but she doesn't know where it is coming from,' Richard explained.

'Hello. It's Finn. We met on our dragons,' said Finn clearly. Suddenly the girl smiled.

'Hello Finn. Where are you?'

'I'm on Sirius using a tele-link,' the boy responded, feeling that this was all a bit surreal. Si was telling the others to touch the watch-com and their throats and foreheads too so they could join in the meeting. They did so and spoke to Tara as well. Ash-ting was watching Tara. He meowed and Tara smiled. 'Ash-ting says hi too,' she said and that broke the ice. She even introduced them to the elf and to Marigold, a fairy, and Eeny the imp, who was now known as Hercules because he had bravely saved Tara from an angry escaped bull.

In return they told her about Blake's operation and all they had done on Sirius. They agreed to keep in touch.

CHAPTER 19

TARA'S GRANDDAD AND THE TELE-LINK

When the link was cut Tara leaned against the oak tree and thought about what had happened. She did get premonitions sometimes and hated it because grown-ups thought she was imagining it if she told them. And also because there was usually nothing she could do about them.

And at that very moment she had a flash of her grandfather lying on the floor groaning. It was very vivid and real. Tara felt herself shrivel inside. What could she do? He lived hundreds of miles away in Scotland. Maybe she was just imagining it – but she still had the horrid feeling inside.

And then she knew she must contact Finn. He would know what to do. She tried to remember his face from the battle of the dragons. She thought of his blond hair and green eyes and his voice and suddenly she could hear him saying, 'Hello Tara. Is that you?'

She told him what had happened. He told her to think about her grandfather and they would connect to him with the tele-link. Moments later all the children could see and hear the elderly man lying on the floor groaning. Si took over. He asked Tara for her grandfather's address – luckily, it was fresh in her memory as she and her family had stayed with him in the recent summer holidays. Then he tele-linked the local ambulance service and requested help.

It was only when Tara's grandfather was safely in hospital and recovering that everyone around him started to wonder who had called the ambulance – and in any case, however did anyone know the old man had fallen? He had been at home alone.

'Life is very strange,' said Tara's mother as she kissed her daughter goodnight.

Tara said nothing.

Miles away Agapay was dreaming about the colourful clothes of the future.

Richard was contemplating how to upgrade the tele-link.

Vaz was imagining himself racing round in a super-fast transport.

And Finn in his bedroom, surrounded by his familiar toys and games, his family downstairs, was fast asleep.

The Magical Adventures of Tara
and The Talking Kitten Series
by Diana Cooper

This children's series by Diana Cooper tells the heartwarming story of a girl and her magic cat. Before Tara meets Ash-ting, an adorable grey kitten, her life at both home and school is dreadful; she doesn't know how to make friends or how to talk to her dad about things that are bothering her. But then Ash-ting enters her life and turns everything around, for Ash-ting is more than just a pet—he can talk!

The Magical Adventures of
Tara and the Talking Kitten

ISBN 978-1-84409-550-6

Tara and the Talking Kitten
Meet Angels and Fairies

ISBN 978-1-84409-551-3

Tara and the Talking Kitten
Meet a Unicorn

ISBN 978-1-84409-557-5

Tara and the Talking Kitten
Meet a Mermaid

ISBN 978-1-84409-580-3

TARA AND HER TALKING KITTEN
MEET THE NAUGHTY DRAGON (CD)
ISBN 978-1-84409-579-7

TARA AND HER TALKING KITTEN
MEET HER GUARDIAN ANGEL (CD)
ISBN 978-1-84409-578-0

Each CD with six delightful stories featuring Tara and her talking kitten Ash-ting. For children aged 5–9 years. Duration: 1 hour approx. each. Written and read by Diana Cooper.

COLOR YOUR LIFE WITH CRYSTALS
BY MARGARET ANN LEMBO

Tapping into children's seemingly inherent love of rocks, this accessible introduction to gemology provides youngsters with a base understanding of crystal qualities, the power of colors, and the metaphysical importance of positive thinking. Divided into seven sections, each chakra is explored and visualization exercises are included in order to experience the chakra's energy. Each crystal has a photograph and text describing its appearance and energy qualities, as well as concrete examples of life situations where a crystal and some positive thought affirmations can be helpful.

ISBN 978-1-84409-605-3

F I N D H O R N   P R E S S

Life-Changing Books

Consult our catalogue online
(with secure order facility) on
www.findhornpress.com

For information on the Findhorn Foundation:
www.findhorn.org